FÜN學

美國各學科初級課本

新生入門英語閱讀 二版

AMERiCAN SCHOOL TEXTBOOK

Reading Key BASIC

American School Textbook
Reading Key
Basic

The Best Preparation for Building Academic Reading Skills and Vocabulary

The Reading Key series is designed to help students to understand American school textbooks and to develop background knowledge in a wide variety of academic topics. This series also provides learners with the opportunity to enhance their reading comprehension skills and vocabulary.

○ **Reading Key** <**Basic 1–4**> is a four-book series designed for beginning learners.

○ **Reading Key** <**Volume 1–3**> is a three-book series designed for beginner to intermediate learners.

○ **Reading Key** <**Volume 4–6**> is a three-book series designed for intermediate to high-intermediate learners.

○ **Reading Key** <**Volume 7–9**> is a three-book series designed for high-intermediate learners.

Features

• A wide variety of topics that cover American school subjects

• Intensive practice for reading skill development

• Building vocabulary through school subjects and themed texts

• Graphic organizers for each passage

• Captivating pictures and illustrations related to the topics

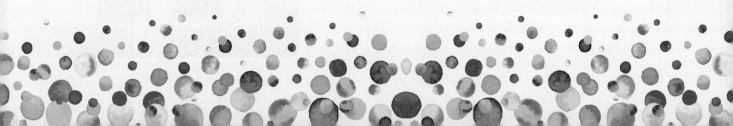

Table of Contents

Component

• Workbook

Syllabus Vol. 2

Subject	Topic & Area	Title
Social Studies ★ **History and Geography**	Culture Culture & History Geography Geography	Special Days The First Thanksgiving What Is a Map? The Oceans and Continents
Science	A World of Plants A World of Plants A World of Animals A World of Animals	Where Do Plants Live? Amazing Plants What Lives in an Ocean? How Frogs Grow and Change
Language ★ **Mathematics** ★ **Visual Arts** ★ **Music**	Reading Stories Numbers and Counting Visual Arts A World of Music	The Three Little Pigs Skip-Counting Colors Musical Instruments and Their Families

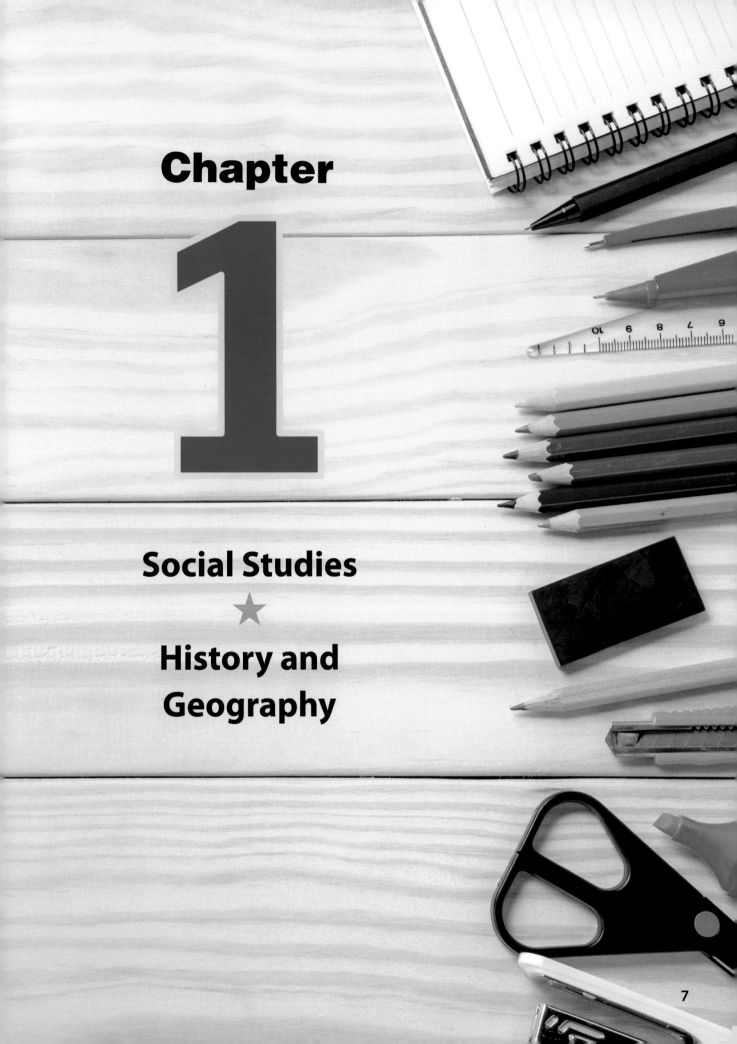

Chapter

1

Social Studies

★

History and Geography

Unit 01

Special Days

Reading Focus

- What are some special days?
- Why do we celebrate special days?
- What special things do we do on special days?

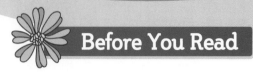

Key Words

birthday

Families' Special Days

Children's Day

Mother's Day

Father's Day

Christmas

Holidays

Thanksgiving

New Year's Day

Independence Day

Power Verbs

have a party
Let's **have** a birthday **party**.

celebrate
We **celebrate** Christmas.

share
We **share** special food.

honor
Americans **honor** Independence Day.

Word Families : Special Days

birthday

cake
candle
present

Christmas

gift
Christmas tree
Santa Claus

Independence Day

parade
fireworks
picnic

Special Days

Tim is having a party today.
His friends are coming to his house.
They will give him presents.
Everyone will have cake and ice cream.
What is this special day?
It's Tim's birthday.

▲ birthday party

There are many special days.
We celebrate special days every year.

Many families celebrate birthdays with a cake.
Children's Day is a special day for children.
Mother's Day is a special day for mothers.
Father's Day is a special day for fathers.

There are also many national holidays.
The entire country celebrates these days.

▲ Mother's Day

Christmas is one important holiday.
People give each other gifts on that day.

Thanksgiving is another big holiday.
Americans share special food with their
family and friends.

▲ Thanksgiving

Americans also honor Independence Day.
They celebrate the country's birthday
with parades and fireworks.

▲ Independence Day parade

Check Understanding

1 **Which special day does each picture show?**

a

b

_____   _____

2 **Many families celebrate birthdays with a _____ .**
a cake   b presents   c ice cream

3 **How often do we celebrate holidays?**
a every day   b every month   c every year

4 **_____ is a special day for mothers.**
a Mother's Day   b Father's Day   c Children's Day

• **Answer the questions below.**

1 What is a special day for children?
⇨ _____ _____ is a special day for children.

2 How do Americans celebrate Independence Day?
⇨ They celebrate it with _____ and _____ .

13

Vocabulary and Grammar Builder

A **Look, Read, and Write.**
Look at the pictures. Write the correct words.

Thanksgiving   celebrate   honor   gifts

1 ▸ People _____ birthdays with cakes.

2 ▸ Americans share special foods on _____.

3 ▸ Americans _____ Independence Day.

4 ▸ People give each other _____ on Christmas.

B **Have or Having?**
Draw a circle around the right words and then write the words.

1   Tim is _____ a party today.
         have   having

2   His friends are _____ to his house.
             come   coming

3   They will _____ him presents.
           give   giving

4   Everyone will _____ cake and ice cream.
             have   having

Unit 02

The First Thanksgiving

📖 **Reading Focus**

- When was the first Thanksgiving?
- Who were the Pilgrims?
- Who helped the Pilgrims?

Key Words

Pilgrims

religion

The First Thanksgiving

Mayflower

Native American

festival

Thanksgiving Foods

turkey

pumpkin pie

Power Verbs

gather together
Families **gather together** on Thanksgiving.

sail
The Pilgrims **sailed** to America.

land in
The Pilgrims **landed in** America.

die
Many people **died** during the winter.

stay with
He **stayed with** the Pilgrims.

thank
They **thanked** God.

Word Families : Actions

fish

hunt

how to

grow food

speak English

The First Thanksgiving

Thanksgiving is a big holiday in America.
Families gather together and have a special meal.

The first Thanksgiving was celebrated by the Pilgrims.
The Pilgrims were a group of people from England.
They went to America for their religion.

They sailed on a ship called the *Mayflower*.
Two months later, they finally landed in America.
It was the winter of 1620.

The winter was very cold and snowy.
Almost half of the Pilgrims died during the winter.

In spring, they met some Native Americans.
They helped the Pilgrims.
One Native American, Squanto, could speak English.
Squanto stayed with the Pilgrims to help them.
He showed them how to fish.
He showed them how to hunt.
He showed them how to grow food.

▲ Families in America have a special meal on Thanksgiving.

▲ The first Thanksgiving was celebrated by the Pilgrims.

Winter, 1620	Spring, 1621	Fall, 1621
The Pilgrims went to America.	They met the Native Americans.	They had a big meal.

That fall, the Pilgrims had lots of food.
The Pilgrims thanked God.
They thanked the Native Americans, too.
They made a big meal.
They invited the Native Americans to their meal.
For three days, they had a big festival.
That was the first Thanksgiving.

Check Understanding

1 Which event does each picture show? Fill in the blanks.

a  b

The _____ went to America.   They met the _____ _____.

2 The Pilgrims were a group of people from _____.

a America   b England   c Canada

3 Who was Squanto?

a a Pilgrim   b a fisherman   c a Native American

4 Why did the Pilgrims invite the Native Americans to their meal?

a to fish   b to grow food   c to thank them

• **Answer the questions below.**

1 How did the Pilgrims go to America?
  ⇨ They sailed on the _____.

2 How did Squanto help the Pilgrims?
  ⇨ He showed them how to _____, _____, and _____ food.

A **Look, Read, and Write.**
Look at the pictures. Write the correct words.

 Native Americans   *Mayflower*   big meal   religion

1 ▸ The Pilgrims sailed on the _____ .

2 ▸ The Pilgrims went to America for their _____ .

3 ▸ The _____ _____ helped the Pilgrims.

4 ▸ They had a _____ .

B **Sailed or Landed?**
Draw a circle around the right words and then write the words.

1 The Pilgrims _____ in America.
        sailed   landed

2 Squanto _____ with the Pilgrims.
        showed   stayed

3 The Pilgrims _____ the Native Americans.
        thanked   sailed

4 The Pilgrims _____ the Native Americans.
        stayed   invited

Unit 03

What Is a Map?

Reading Focus

- What is a map?
- Why do people use maps?
- What are the four main directions?

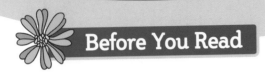 **Before You Read**

 05

Key Words

Maps

world map

country map

city map

neighborhood map

Directions

North

West

East

South

Power Verbs

show
A map **shows** many places.

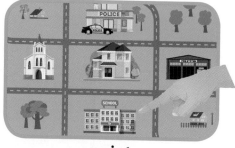

point
Point to the school on the map.

find
Can you **find** the school?

follow
Just **follow** the arrow.

Word Families : Places

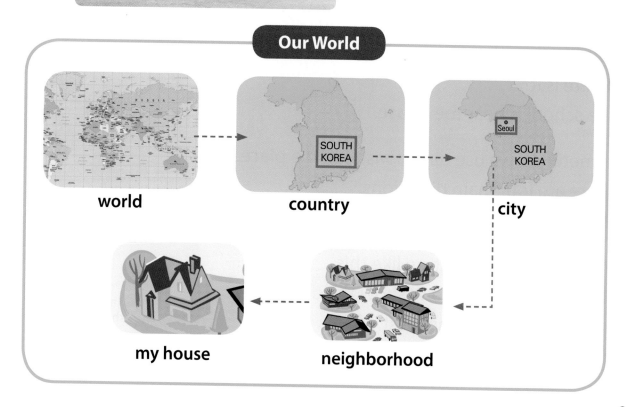

Our World

world

country

city

my house

neighborhood

What Is a Map?

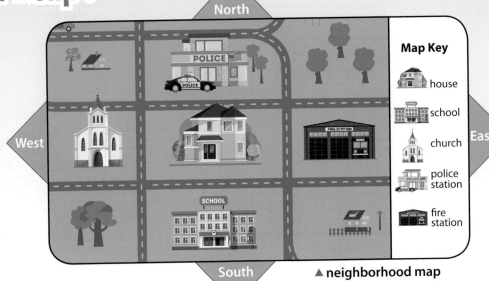

▲ neighborhood map

Look at the map.
You can see many houses, trees, and buildings.

A map is a drawing of a real place.
A map can show many places.
It can show the entire world.
It can show a country or a city.
Or it can just show a small neighborhood.

A map helps you know where things are.
Point to the school on the map.
Where is it?
The school is near the house.

Sometimes, we use directions to find a place.
There are four main directions.
They are north, south, east, and west.

Many maps use a picture like this.
The letters N, S, E, and W show the directions:
north, south, east, and west.
If you follow the arrow, you can go that direction.

The letters show
the directions.

Now, look at the map again.

Where is the school?

The school is south of the house.

The police station is north of the house.

The fire station is east of the house.

The church is west of the house.

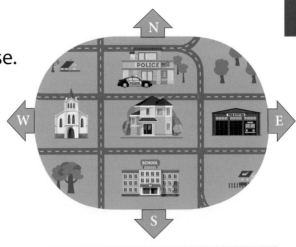

Check Understanding

1 Which type of map does each picture show?

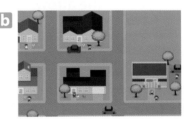

a map of the _____   a map of a _____

2 A _____ helps you know where things are.
   a building   **b** map   **c** park

3 Sometimes, we use _____ to find a place.
   a trees   **b** pictures   **c** directions

4 East and west are _____.
   a directions   **b** places   **c** maps

• **Answer the questions below.**

1 What are the four main directions?
   ⇨ They are _____, _____, _____, and _____.

2 What can a map show?
   ⇨ It can show the entire _____ or just a small _____.

25

Vocabulary and Grammar Builder

A **Look, Read, and Write.**
Look at the pictures. Write the correct words.

point   show   find   follow

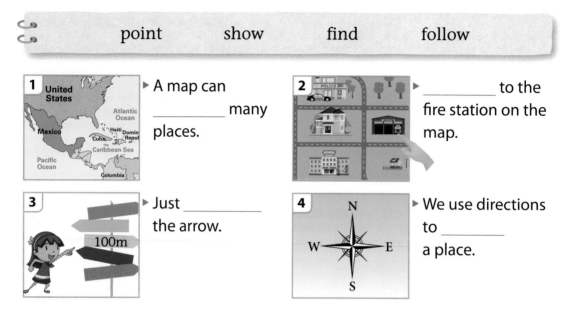

1 United States
▶ A map can _____ many places.

2
▶ _____ to the fire station on the map.

3
▶ Just _____ the arrow.

4
N W E S
▶ We use directions to _____ a place.

B **North or South?**
Draw a circle around the right words and then write the words.

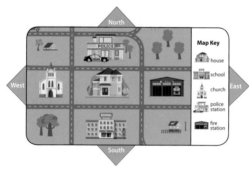

1 The police station is _____ of the house.
south   north

2 The school is _____ of the house.
south   north

3 The church is _____ of the house.
east   west

4 The fire station is _____ of the house.
east   west

26

Unit 04

The Oceans and Continents

Reading Focus

- What is a continent?
- What is an ocean?
- What continent do you live on?

Before You Read

 07

Key Words

Seven Continents

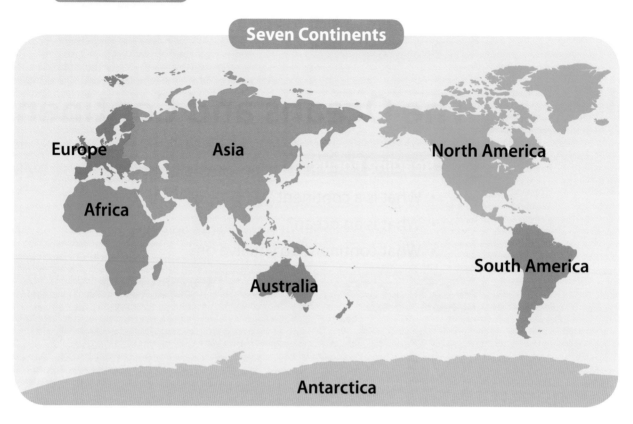

Europe

Asia

North America

Africa

South America

Australia

Antarctica

Five Oceans

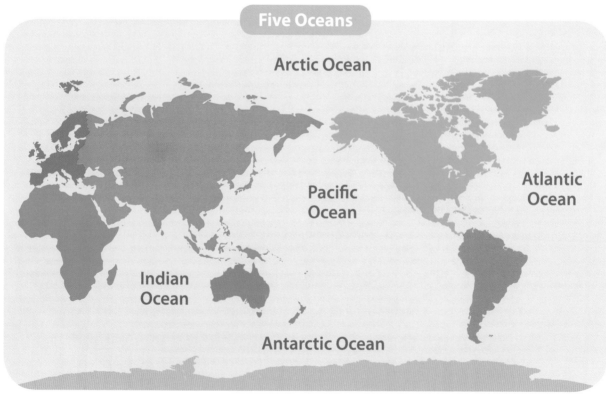

Arctic Ocean

Pacific Ocean

Atlantic Ocean

Indian Ocean

Antarctic Ocean

Power Verbs

be made up of
Earth is made up of continents and oceans.

be located in
Korea is located in Asia.

be connected to
China is connected to Russia.

be surrounded by
An island is surrounded by water.

Word Families : Positions

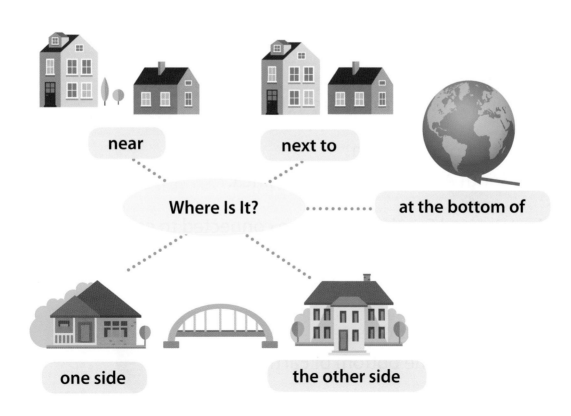

near

next to

Where Is It?

at the bottom of

one side

the other side

29

Arctic Ocean

Europe   Asia   North America   Atlantic Ocean

Africa   Pacific Ocean

Indian Ocean

Australia   South America

Antarctic Ocean

Antarctica

The Oceans and Continents

Look at the map of the world.
Earth is made up of continents and oceans.

A continent is a very large body of land.
There are seven continents on Earth.
An ocean is a very large body of water.
There are five oceans on Earth.

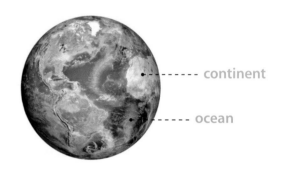

continent

ocean

We live on a continent.
Asia is the largest continent.
Russia, China, Korea, and Japan are in Asia.

Europe is next to Asia.
England, France, and Germany are in Europe.

Africa is near Europe and Asia.
Egypt and South Africa are located in Africa.

North America and South America are connected to each other.
The United States and Canada are located in North America.
Brazil and Argentina are located in South America.

Australia is an island continent.
And Antarctica is at the bottom of Earth.

Australia

Antarctica

The continents are surrounded by the oceans.
The Pacific Ocean is the biggest ocean.
Asia is on one side of it.
North and South America are
on the other side of it.

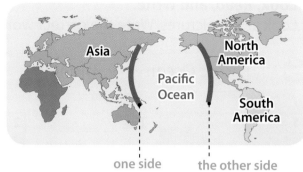

one side   the other side

Check Understanding

1   Which continent does each picture show?

_____   _____

2   What is a continent?
  a a large body of land   b a large body of ocean
  c a large body of water

3   Which country is in Africa?
  a Korea   b England   c Egypt

4   Antarctica is at the _____ of Earth.
  a top   b side   c bottom

• Answer the questions below.

1 What two things is Earth made up of?
  ⇨ Earth is made up of _____ and _____.

2 Name the seven continents on Earth.
  ⇨ They are _____, _____, Africa, _____ _____,
    South America, Australia , and _____.

Vocabulary and Grammar Builder

A **Look, Read, and Write.**
Look at the pictures. Write the correct words.

Pacific Ocean	island	Asia	South America

1 ▸ The _____ _____ is the biggest ocean.

2 ▸ Korea and Japan are located in _____.

3 ▸ Brazil and Argentina are in _____ _____.

4 ▸ Australia is an _____ continent.

B **Next or Next To?**
Draw a circle around the right words and then write the words.

1 Europe is _____ Asia.
   next   next to

2 The continents are _____ water.
   surround   surrounded by

3 The United States is _____ North America.
   locate   located in

4 North and South America are _____ each other.
   connect   connected to

A Look at the pictures. Write the correct words.

national holidays   real   bottom   Pilgrims

1  ▶ The entire country celebrates _____ .

2  ▶ The native Americans helped the _____ .

3  ▶ A map is a drawing of a _____ place.

4  ▶ Antarctica is at the _____ of Earth.

B Draw a circle around the right words and then write the words.

  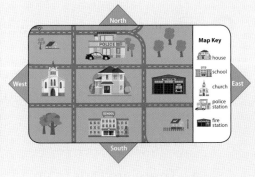

1 Tim is _____ a party today.
      have   having

2 Squanto _____ the Pilgrims how to hunt.
      showed   stayed

3 The fire station is _____ of the house.
      east   west

4 The school is _____ of the house.
      north   south

C Complete the sentences with the words below.

| each other | celebrate | honor | entire |
| festival | Thanksgiving | stayed | invited |

1 We _____ special days every year.

2 The _____ country celebrates national holidays.

3 People give _____ gifts on Christmas.

4 Americans _____ Independence Day.

5 The first _____ was celebrated by the Pilgrims.

6 Squanto _____ with the Pilgrims to help them.

7 The Pilgrims _____ the Native Americans to their meal.

8 For three days, they had a big _____.

D Complete the sentences with the words below.

| arrow | directions | east | connected |
| show | oceans | Asia | continents |

1 A map can _____ many places.

2 There are four main _____.

3 They are north, south, _____, and west.

4 If you follow the _____, you can go that direction.

5 There are seven _____ on Earth.

6 There are five _____ on Earth.

7 _____ is the largest continent.

8 North America and South America are _____ to each other.

Chapter

2

Science

Unit 05

Where Do Plants Live?

Reading Focus

- What kinds of plants grow in rainforests?
- What kinds of plants grow in deserts?
- What kinds of plants grow in tundra?

Key Words

forest

rainforest

Places to Live

desert

grassland

tundra

oak tree

maple tree

Types of Plants

fern

wildflower

cactus

Power Verbs

get rain
Rainforests **get** lots of **rain**.

store
Desert plants **store** water.

hold
Plants' roots **hold** water.

survive
Plants can **survive** in the cold.

Word Families : Living Places

rainforest ➡ hot and wet

desert ➡ hot and dry

tundra ➡ cold and snowy

grassland ➡ covered with grass

Where Do Plants Live?

▼ rainforest plants

forest floor

▲ Many plants live in rainforests.

Plants live in many places.

Many plants live in rainforests.
A rainforest is a hot, wet place.
It gets lots of rain.

There are many tall trees in a rainforest.
They often have large leaves.
Below the tall trees, there are smaller plants.
Ferns and flowers grow on the forest floor.

Some plants live in deserts.
A desert is a hot, dry place.
It gets very little rain.
How do plants grow in such a hot
and dry place?

▲ desert plants

Many desert plants have thick stems.
These help the plants store water.
A cactus is a desert plant.
It can hold water in its thick stem.
So it can use the water later
if it does not rain for a long time.

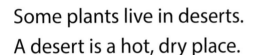
◀ A cactus can hold
water in its thick stem.

Some plants even live in the tundra.
Tundra is a cold, snowy place.
Plants there do not grow very tall.
And they grow close together.
This helps them survive in the cold tundra.

▲ Plants in the tundra are not tall.

Check Understanding

1 **Which place does each picture show?**

a

b

_____   _____

2 **Which place gets very little rain?**
   a a rainforest   b a desert   c a tundra

3 **How is the weather in the tundra?**
   a cold and dry   b hot and wet   c cold and snowy

4 **A cactus holds water in its thick _____.**
   a root   b stem   c leaves

- **Answer the questions below.**

1 What do the trees in rainforests look like?
   ⇨ They are _____ and have _____ leaves.

2 How can plants grow in a hot and dry desert?
   ⇨ They can store _____ in their _____ _____.

41

Vocabulary and Grammar Builder

A **Look, Read, and Write.**
Look at the pictures. Write the correct words.

> tundra   deserts   ferns   rainforests

1 _____ ▶ get lots of rain.

2 ▶ _____ get very little rain.

3 ▶ _____ grow on the forest floor.

4 ▶ Plants in the _____ are not tall.

B **Dry or Wet?**
Draw a circle around the right words and then write the words.

1   A rainforest is a hot, _____ place.
       dry   wet

2   Plants in rainforests have _____ leaves.
       small   large

3   The stem of a cactus is _____.
       thick   thin

4   Tundra is a cold, _____ place.
       sunny   snowy

Unit 06

Amazing Plants

Reading Focus

- What is the world's tallest plant?
- What is the world's biggest flower?
- What are some insect-eating plants?

Before You Read

Key Words

Amazing Plants

redwood tree
the world's tallest tree

rafflesia
the world's biggest flower

Insect-Eating Plants

Venus flytrap

long spine

sundew plant

sticky hairs

pitcher plant

cup-shaped leaf

Power Verbs

catch
Some plants **catch** insects.

land on
Insects **land on** the leaf.

trap
The leaf **traps** the insect.

be covered with
The leaf **is covered with** hairs.

look like
The leaf **looks like** a pitcher.

fall into
Insects **fall into** the hole.

Word Families

amazing

tall

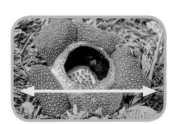

wide

sticky

cup-shaped

pitcher

45

redwood

Amazing Plants

There are more than 300,000 types of plants.
Some plants are amazing.

The redwood tree is the tallest tree in the world.
It grows in California in the U.S.A.
Some redwoods can grow more than 100 meters tall.

The rafflesia is the biggest flower in the world.
It grows in the jungles of Asia.
This flower can be more than one meter wide.

Some plants catch insects.
They are insect-eating plants.

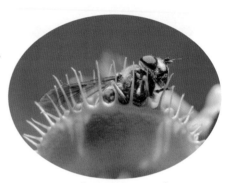
▲ an insect trapped in the leaf

The Venus flytrap has special leaves.
The leaves hold a sweet juice.
An insect lands on the leaf.
Then, the leaf quickly closes.
The leaf traps the insect.
Then, juices from the plant digest it.

The sundew plant has special leaves, too.
The leaves are covered with sticky hairs.
An insect lands on the sticky hairs.
Then, the leaf slowly closes.
Then, juices from the plant digest it.

▲ an insect on a sundew plant

Pitcher plants have leaves that look like pitchers.
Splash! Insects fall into the cup-shaped leaves.
Then, juices from the plant digest them.

▶ Pitcher plants have
cup-shaped leaves.

Check Understanding

1 **Which plant does each picture show?**

a

b

_____   _____

2 **Which plant can be more than one meter wide?**
  a a redwood   b a pitcher plant   c a rafflesia

3 **Which plant can catch insects?**
  a a rafflesia   b a redwood   c a Venus flytrap

4 **The leaves of a sundew plant have many _____ hairs.**
  a juicy   b sticky   c large

• **Answer the questions below.**

1 What is the world's tallest tree?
⇨ The _____ _____ is the _____ _____ in the world.

2 What are some insect-eating plants?
⇨ They are the Venus flytrap, _____ _____, and
_____ _____.

Vocabulary and Grammar Builder

A **Look, Read, and Write.**
Look at the pictures. Write the correct words.

> trap   fall   digest   land

1 ▸ The leaves of a Venus flytrap _____ insects.

3 ▸ Insects _____ into the cup-shaped leaf.

2 ▸ Insects _____ on the sticky hairs.

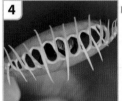
4 ▸ Juices from the plant _____ the insect.

B **Wide or Tall?**
Draw a circle around the right words and then write the words.

1   Insect-eating plants are _____.
        amaze   amazing

2   The redwood tree can grow more than100 meters _____.
        tall   wide

3   The rafflesia is the _____ flower in the world.
        big   biggest

4   The pitcher plant has _____ leaves.
        cup-shaped   cup-shape

Unit

07

What Lives in an Ocean?

Reading Focus

- What are some ocean animals?
- How are these ocean animals alike?
- How are sharks special?

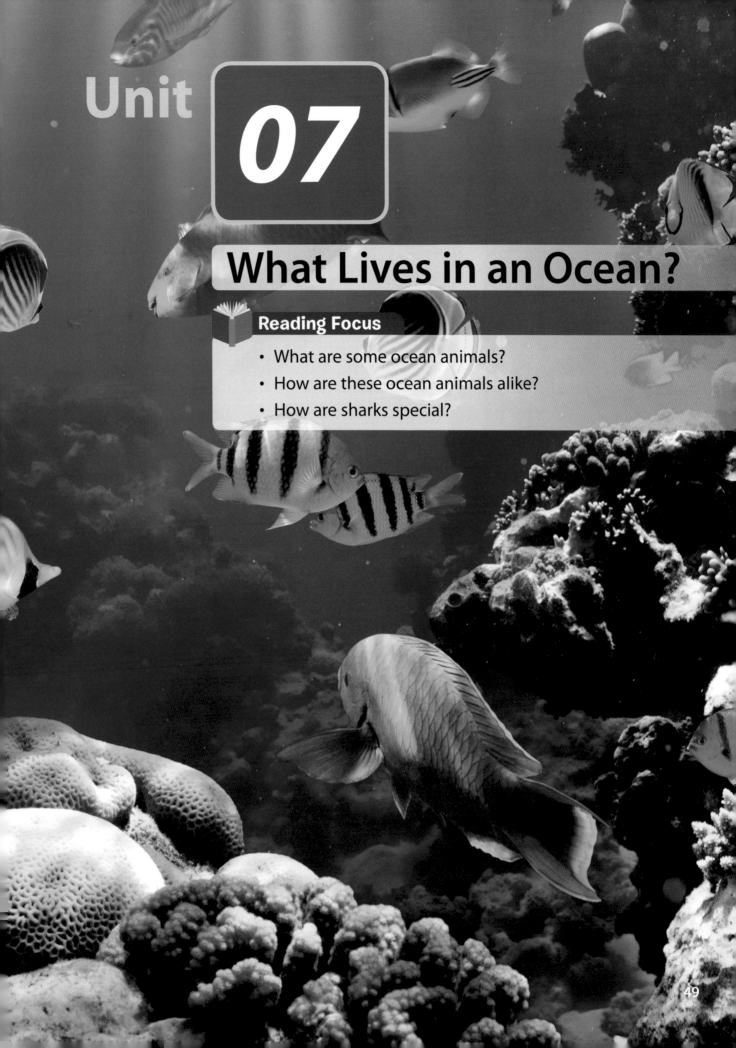

Key Words

dolphin

shark

whale

Ocean Animals

crab

lobster

sea turtle

A Shark's Body Parts

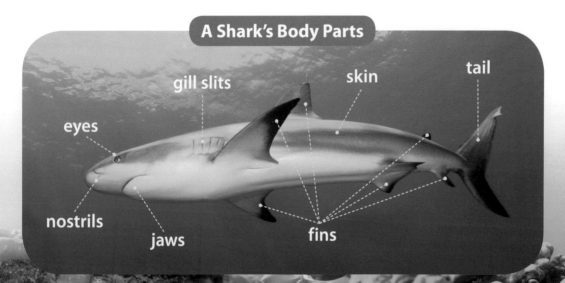

gill slits

skin

tail

eyes

nostrils

jaws

fins

Power Verbs

breathe
Fish **breathe** in water.

take a close look at
Let's **take a close look at** a shark.

hunt
Sharks **hunt** fish.

attack
Great white sharks **attack** people.

Word Families : A Shark's Body Parts

Sharks are special.

fins ➡ Sharks have large and long fins.

tail ➡ Some sharks have a very long tail.

jaws ➡ Sharks' jaws have many sharp teeth.

nostrils ➡ Sharks use their nostrils to smell.

What Lives in an Ocean?

14

An ocean is a very large sea.
Many plants and animals live in the ocean.
Fish, crabs, sea turtles, sharks, and dolphins are all ocean animals.

All fish live in water and have gills.
Gills help fish breathe in water.

Fish have fins and tails, too.
They use their fins and tails to swim.

tail

gills

fins

Look at the sharks!
Are they fish?
Yes, sharks are fish, but they are special.
Let's take a close look at a shark.

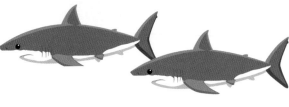

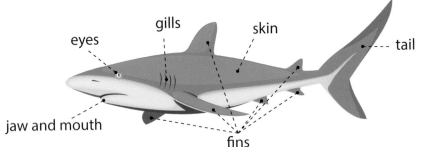

eyes
gills
skin
tail
jaw and mouth
fins

Sharks have large and long fins.
These fins and tails help sharks swim fast.

Sharks have large jaws with very sharp teeth.
The sharp teeth help sharks hunt fish well.

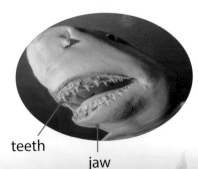

teeth

jaw

Sharks can see well in the blue water.
Sharks can hear sounds from far away.
Sharks use their nostrils to smell.

There are more than five hundred kinds of sharks.
Some sharks are very dangerous.
The great white shark is the most dangerous shark.
It attacks anything—even people!

nostril

▲ The great white shark is
the most dangerous shark.

Check Understanding

1 Which ocean animal does each picture show?

a

b

_____   _____

2 What do all fish have?
a big tails   b gills   c sharp teeth

3 What helps sharks swim fast?
a gills and tails   b fins and teeth   c fins and tails

4 Sharks use their _____ to smell.
a fins   b jaws   c nostrils

• Answer the questions below.

1 What are some ocean animals?
⇨ They are _____, _____, _____ _____, sharks, and _____.

2 Which shark is the most dangerous?
⇨ The _____ _____ _____ is the most dangerous shark.

A **Look, Read, and Write.**
Look at the pictures. Write the correct words.

> attack   gills   hunt   fins

1 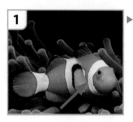 ▸ _____ help fish breathe in water.

2  ▸ Fish use their _____ to swim.

3  ▸ Sharks _____ other ocean animals.

4  ▸ The great white shark can _____ people.

B **What Body Parts?**
Draw a circle around the right words and then write the words.

1   Sharks have large _____.
     nostrils   jaws

2   Sharks' large and long _____ help them swim fast.
     gills   fins

3   Sharks' sharp _____ help them hunt well.
     mouth   teeth

4   Sharks use their _____ to smell.
     nostrils   gills

Unit 08

How Frogs Grow and Change

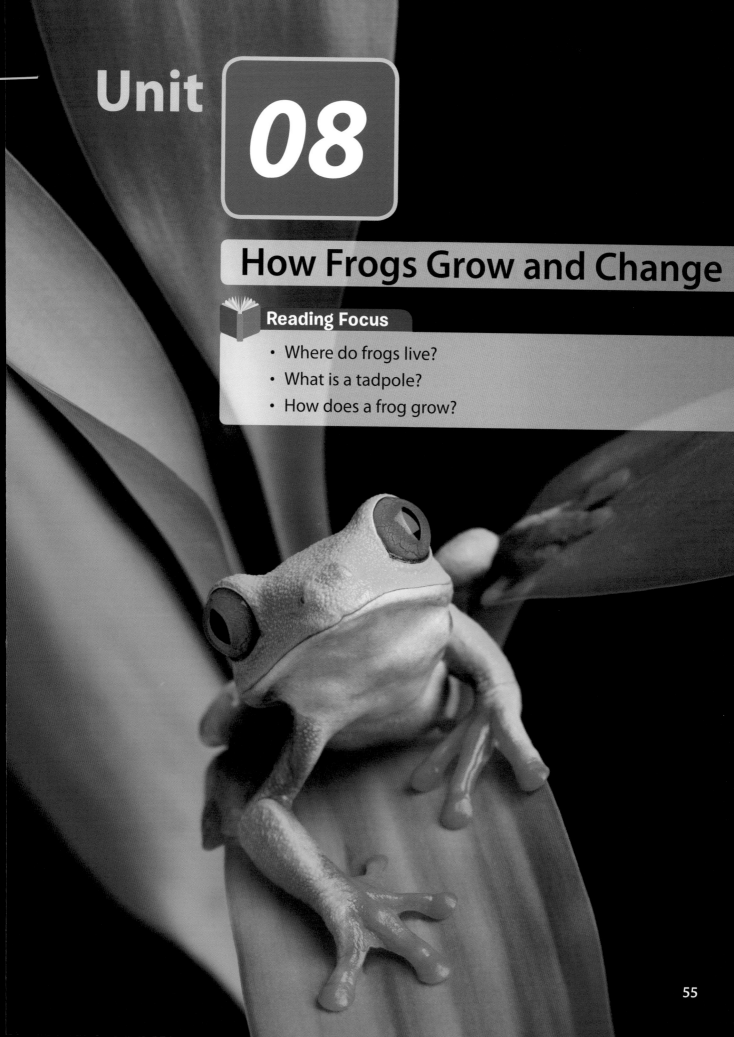

Reading Focus

- Where do frogs live?
- What is a tadpole?
- How does a frog grow?

Before You Read

Key Words

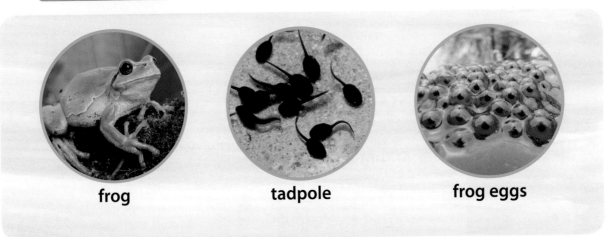

frog   tadpole   frog eggs

A Frog's Body Parts

eyes

skin

tongue

back legs

front legs

webbed feet

Power Verbs

leap
Frogs can **leap** high.

frog
tadpole

look different
Frogs and tadpoles
look different.

lay eggs
Frogs **lay eggs.**

hatch
Tadpoles **hatch** from eggs.

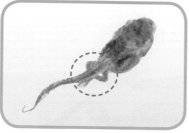

develop
Tadpoles **develop** legs.

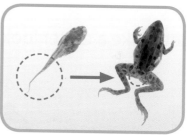

disappear
Tadpoles' tails **disappear.**

Word Families : Frog's Habitats

pond

swamp

Where Frogs Live

lake

land

How Frogs Grow and Change

Ribbit, ribbit, ribbit.
Can you hear the frogs?

Frogs live in many places.
They live in ponds, swamps, and lakes.
They also live on land.
Frogs can live both on land and in the water.

Let's take a closer look at a frog.

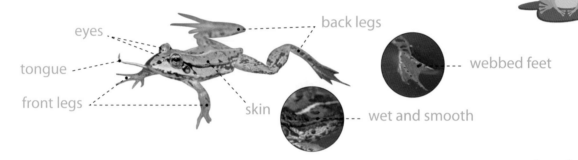

eyes

tongue

front legs

back legs

webbed feet

skin

wet and smooth

Frogs have long back legs. These help frogs leap well.
Frogs have webbed feet. These help frogs swim well.
Frogs have wet, smooth skin.
And frogs can catch bugs with their long tongues.

But they do not always look like that.
As babies, frogs look very different.

What is this?
It is a tadpole. It's a baby frog.

Frogs lay eggs in winter.
Tadpoles hatch from the eggs.

▲ frog eggs

Tadpoles only live in the water.
They have long tails like fish.

Gradually, tadpoles develop legs.
Their tails slowly disappear.
After a few weeks,
they become adult frogs.
Then, they can live on land.

frog eggs

tadpole
(after 2 weeks)

adult frog
(after 14 weeks)

(after 7 weeks)

▲ Frogs grow and change.

Check Understanding

1 **Which body part does each picture show?**

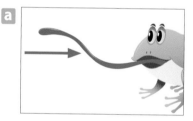

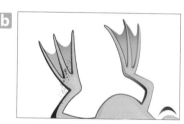

_____   _____

2 **Where can frogs live?**
   a only on land   b only in the water   c on land and in the water

3 **How do frogs use their long back legs?**
   a to swim well   b to catch bugs   c to leap well

4 **A _____ is a baby frog.**
   a tadpole   b bug   c tail

• **Answer the questions below.**

1 When do frogs lay eggs? ⇨ Frogs lay eggs in _____.

2 How do frogs use their long tongues?
   ⇨ Frogs _____ _____ with their long tongues.

Vocabulary and Grammar Builder

A **Look, Read, and Write.**
Look at the pictures. Write the correct words.

| catch bugs | ponds | tadpoles | leap |

 **1** ▸ Frogs live in _____, lakes, and swamps.

 **2** ▸ Frogs can _____ high.

 **3** ▸ Frogs _____ _____ with their long tongues.

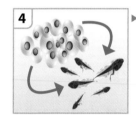 **4** ▸ _____ hatch from eggs.

B **Dry or Wet?**
Draw a circle around the right words and then write the words.

1 Frogs have _____ skin.
dry   wet

2 Frogs have _____ feet.
web   webbed

3 Frogs also have wet, _____ skin.
smooth   webbed

4 Baby frogs look _____ from adult frogs.
different   alike

60

Review Test 2

A Look at the pictures. Write the correct words.

fins	hatch	catch	hold

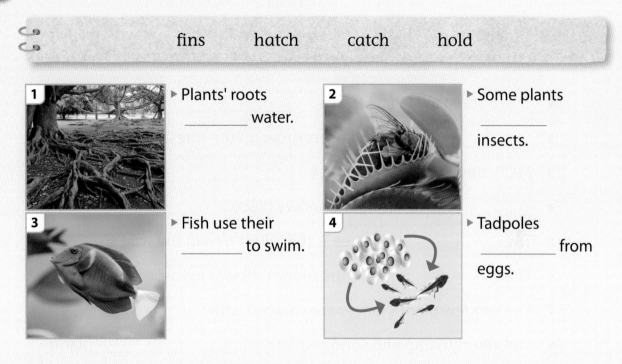

1 ▸ Plants' roots _____ water.

2 ▸ Some plants _____ insects.

3 ▸ Fish use their _____ to swim.

4 ▸ Tadpoles _____ from eggs.

B Draw a circle around the right words and then write the words.

1 Tundra is a _____ place.
sunny   snowy

2 The rafflesia can be more than one meter _____.
tall   wide

3 Sharks have large _____.
nostrils   jaws

4 Frogs and tadpoles look _____.
alike   different

C Complete the sentences with the words below.

stems	sticky	tundra	redwood
insect-eating	ferns	rainforest	rafflesia

1 There are many tall trees in a _____.

2 _____ and flowers grow on the forest floor.

3 Many desert plants have thick _____.

4 _____ is a cold, snowy place.

5 The _____ tree is the tallest tree in the world.

6 The _____ is the biggest flower in the world.

7 The sundew plant's leaves are covered with _____ hairs.

8 The Venus flytrap and sundew plant are _____ plants.

D Complete the sentences with the words below.

nostrils	on land	webbed	catch bugs
ocean animals	lay eggs	tails	dangerous

1 Fish, crabs, sharks, and dolphins are all _____.

2 Fish use their fins and _____ to swim.

3 Sharks use their _____ to smell.

4 The great white shark is the most _____ shark.

5 Frogs can live both _____ and in the water.

6 Frogs can _____ with their long tongues.

7 Frogs have _____ feet to help them swim well.

8 Frogs _____ in winter.

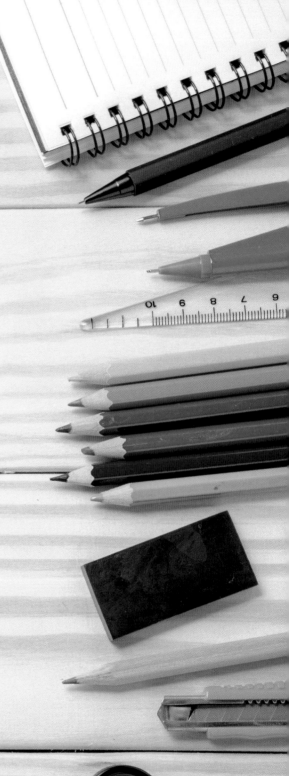

Chapter

3

Language

★

Mathematics

★

Visual Arts

★

Music

Unit 09

The Three Little Pigs

Reading Focus

- What animals appear in the story?
- What did the three little pigs build their houses with?
- What happened to the big bad wolf?

Before You Read

17

Key Words

Who Is in the Story?

the first little pig

the second little pig

the third little pig

the big bad wolf

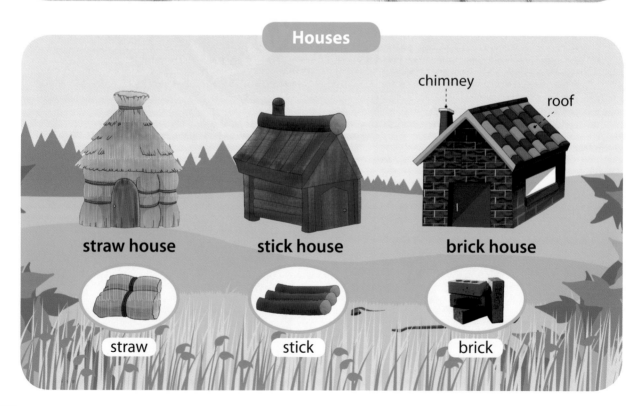

Houses

chimney

roof

straw house

stick house

brick house

straw

stick

brick

Power Verbs

decide to
They **decided to** leave.

build
The little pig **built** a house.

knock
He **knocked** on the door.

huff (= puff)
The wolf **huffed** and **puffed**.

blow down
The wind **blew down** the house.

run away
The wolf **ran away**.

Word Families : Actions

climb up
He **climbed up** on the roof.

jump down
He **jumped down** the chimney.

fall into
He **fell into** the hot water.

scream
He **screamed** loudly.

yell
He **yelled** loudly.

The Three Little Pigs

Once upon a time, there were three little pigs.
One day, they decided to leave home and
make their own houses.

The first little pig built a house with straw.
The second little pig built a house with sticks.
The third little pig built a house with hard bricks.

In the woods, there lived a big bad wolf.
One day, the wolf saw the first little pig in his house of straw.
"Yum, yum, that pig would be yummy,"
thought the big bad wolf.

Soon, the big bad wolf came up to
the house of straw.
He knocked on the door and said,
"Little pig, little pig, let me come in."
The little pig answered,
"No, no! Not by the hair of my chinny chin chin."
"Then I'll huff, and I'll puff, and I'll blow
your house down," said the wolf.
And he huffed and puffed, and
he blew down the house of straw.

The first little pig ran away to the second little pig's house.
He told the second little pig about the big bad wolf.

Just then, the big bad wolf came up to the house of sticks.
He knocked on the door and said,
"Little pig, little pig, let me come in."
"No, no! Not by the hair of my chinny chin chin,"
answered the little pig.
"Then I'll huff, and I'll puff, and I'll blow
your house down," said the wolf.
And he huffed and puffed, and
he blew down the house of sticks.

The two pigs ran away to the third little pig's house.
They told the third little pig about the big bad wolf.

Just then, the big bad wolf came up to the house of bricks.
"Little pig, little pig, let me come in," he said.
"No, no! Not by the hair of my chinny chin chin," answered the
little pig.
Then I'll huff, and I'll puff, and I'll blow your house down," said
the wolf.
So, the wolf huffed and puffed, and he puffed and huffed,
but he couldn't blow down the house of bricks.
"My house is too strong for you to
blow down," said the third little pig.

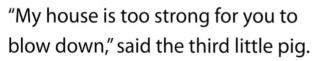

The big bad wolf looked at the brick house.
He saw a chimney on the top.
"Aha," he thought.
"I will climb up on the roof and then
get into the house through the chimney."
"Then, I can eat the three little pigs," he said to himself.
The big bad wolf jumped down the chimney.

But the third little pig was very clever.
He put a big pot of boiling water in the fireplace.
SPLASH!
The big bad wolf fell into the boiling hot water.
He screamed and yelled and ran away.
And the three little pigs lived happily ever after.

1 Which house does each picture show?

 **a**    **b**

_____   _____

2 What did the third little pig build his house with?
a bricks   **b** straw   **c** sticks

3 What did the big bad wolf do to the first and second little pigs' houses?
a He burned them down.
b He blew them down.
c He pushed them down.

4 Whose house was the strongest?
a the first little pig's straw house
b the second little pig's stick house
c the third little pig's brick house

5 The wolf tried to get into the third little pig's house through the
_____.
a chimney   **b** door   **c** window

6 What did the third little pig put in the fireplace?
a a hard brick   **b** a pot of boiling water   **c** a strong stick

• **Answer the questions below.**

1 What did the three little pigs make their houses with?
⇨ They made their houses with _____, _____, and _____.

2 Where did the big bad wolf fall into?
⇨ He _____ _____ a pot of boiling _____ _____.

Vocabulary and Grammar Builder

A **Look, Read, and Write.**
Look at the pictures. Write the correct words.

| boiling | first | sticks | bricks |

1  ▸ The _____ pig built a house with straw.

2  ▸ The second little pig built a house with _____.

3  ▸ The third pig built a house with _____.

4  ▸ The wolf fell into the _____ hot water.

B **Knock or Knocked?**
Draw a circle around the past form of each verb and then write the verb.

1   The big bad wolf _____ on the door. (knock)
　　　　　　　　knocked   knockt

2   The big bad wolf _____ down the house. (blow)
　　　　　　　　blowed   blew

3   The big bad wolf yelled and _____ away. (run)
　　　　　　　　　runned   ran

4   The big bad wolf _____ down the chimney. (jump)
　　　　　　　jumped   jumpped

Unit 10

Skip-Counting

Reading Focus

- What are the numbers from 11 to 20?
- Can you count by twos?
- How many things are in a pair?

19

Key Words

Numbers

1	2	3	4	5
one	two	three	four	five
6	7	8	9	10
six	seven	eight	nine	ten
11	12	13	14	15
eleven	twelve	thirteen	fourteen	fifteen
16	17	18	19	20
sixteen	seventeen	eighteen	nineteen	twenty

Skip-Counting

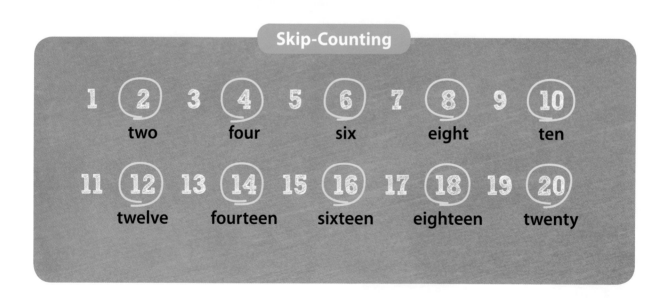

1 ② 3 ④ 5 ⑥ 7 ⑧ 9 ⑩
two   four   six   eight   ten

11 ⑫ 13 ⑭ 15 ⑯ 17 ⑱ 19 ⑳
twelve   fourteen   sixteen   eighteen   twenty

Power Verbs

2, 4, 6, 8, 10

skip-count
Let's **skip-count** by twos.

find out
Let's **find out** the answer.

be grouped
They **are grouped** by twos.

come in
Shoes **come in** pairs.

wear
She is **wearing** a pink dress.

Word Families : Pairs of Things

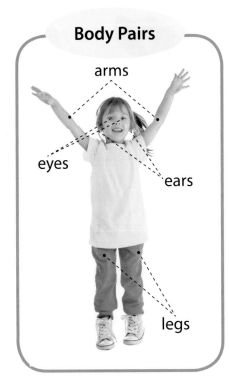

Body Pairs

arms

eyes

ears

legs

Clothing Pairs

pants

socks

shoes

gloves

glasses

Skip-Counting

Let's count to ten.
One, two, three, four, five, six, seven, eight, nine, ten.
We counted them one by one.

Let's count them by twos.
Two, four, six, eight, ten.
Counting by twos is much faster
than counting by ones.

▲ counting by ones

▲ counting by twos

When we count by twos, we are "skip-counting."
Let's skip-count to twenty by twos.
Two, four, six, eight, ten.
Twelve, fourteen, sixteen, eighteen, twenty.

Look at the shoes.
Let's find out how many shoes there are.

They are grouped by twos. We call them a pair.
Can you count them by twos?
2, 4, 6, 8, 10, 12.
How many shoes are there?
There are twelve shoes.
How many pairs of shoes are there?
There are six pairs of shoes.

▲ a pair of shoes

Many things come in groups of twos, or pairs.

You have a pair of eyes.

You have a pair of arms.

You have a pair of legs.

People wear a pair of socks.

People wear a pair of gloves.

Some people wear a pair of glasses.

a pair of arms

a pair of legs

Check Understanding

1   **Which pair does each picture show?**

a

a pair of _____

b

a pair of _____

2   **How many things are in a pair?**

a one   b two   c three

3   **Which numbers are grouped by twos?**

a 1, 2, 3, 4, 5   b 2, 4, 6, 8, 10   c 5, 10, 15, 20, 25

4   **We have a pair of _____.**

a ears   b finger   c mouth

- **Answer the questions below.**

1   What are the numbers from 11 to 15?
   ⇨ They are _____, _____, _____, _____,
      and _____.

2   What are the numbers from 16 to 20?
   ⇨ They are _____, _____, _____, _____,
      and _____.

Vocabulary and Grammar Builder

A **Look, Read, and Write.**
Look at the pictures. Write the correct words.

> skip-count   grouped   come in   pair

1
12, 14, 16, 18, 20
▸ Let's _____ by twos.

2
▸ He has a _____ of gloves.

3
▸ They are _____ by twos.

4
▸ Shoes _____ pairs.

B **One or More?**
Draw a circle around the right words and then write the words.

1   You have a pair of _____.
    eye   eyes

2   You have a pair of _____.
    arm   arms

3   People wear a pair of _____.
    sock   socks

4   Some people wear a pair of _____.
    glass   glasses

78

11

Colors

Reading Focus

- How many colors can you name?
- What are warm colors?
- What are cool colors?

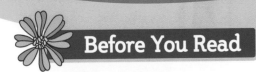

Key Words

Colors

blue

primary colors

green

purple

orange

black   white

orange
red
yellow

warm colors

blue
green
purple

cool colors

cool — — warm

80

Power Verbs

look around
Look around you.

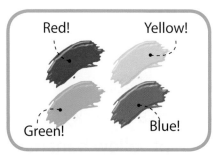

name
Name your favorite color.

mix
Let's mix the colors.

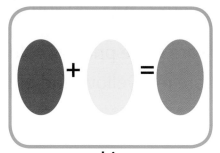

combine
Combine red and yellow.

Word Families : Sensations

exciting
The game is very **exciting**.

excited
I feel **excited** when I play the game.

relaxing
Staying at home is **relaxing**.

relaxed
I feel **relaxed** when I listen
to music.

calm
The sea was very **calm**.

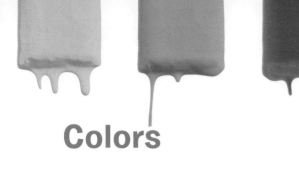

Colors

Look around you.
Do you see a blue sky? Some green grass?
A bunch of yellow bananas?
We can see colors everywhere.
How many colors can you name?

▲ a bunch of bananas

There are three primary colors.
They are red, yellow, and blue.

We can mix the primary colors together.
Then, we can make other colors.

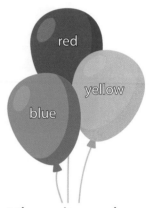

▲ three primary colors

Mix blue and yellow together. You can make green.

Mix blue and red together. You can make purple.

Mix red and yellow together. You can make orange.

Combine red, blue, and yellow together.
Then you can make black.

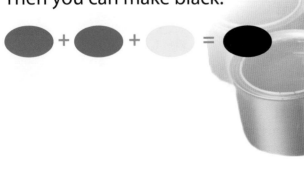

Some colors are "warm."
Red, yellow, and orange are warm colors.
They make us feel excited and happy.

Some colors are "cool."
Blue, green, and purple are cool colors.
They make us feel relaxed.

Do you like warm, exciting colors?
Or do you like cool, calm colors?

cool 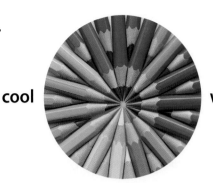 warm

Check Understanding

1 **Which color does each picture show?**

a

b

_____   _____

2 **What is one of the primary colors?**

a green   b red   c black

3 **How do cool colors make people feel?**

a excited   b relaxed   c angry

4 **A _____ color makes people feel excited.**

a hot   b cool   c warm

- **Answer the questions below.**
1 What are the three primary colors?
   ⇨They are _____, _____, and _____.
2 What are some warm colors?
   ⇨They are _____, _____, and _____.

Vocabulary and Grammar Builder

A **Look, Read, and Write.**
Look at the pictures. Write the correct words.

> mix   primary   name   calm

1 ▶ Yellow is a _____ color.

2 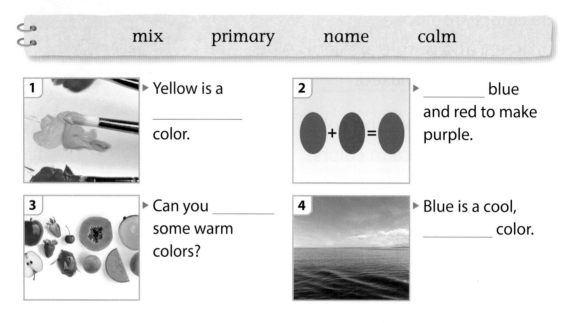 ▶ _____ blue and red to make purple.

3 ▶ Can you _____ some warm colors?

4 ▶ Blue is a cool, _____ color.

B **Excited or Exciting?**
Draw a circle around the right words and then write the words.

1   The game is very _____.
        excited   exciting

2   Warm colors make us feel _____.
        excited   exciting

3   Staying at home is _____.
        relaxing   feel relaxed

4   Cool colors make us feel _____.
        relaxed   relaxing

Unit

12

Musical Instruments and Their Families

Reading Focus

- What are some musical instruments?
- How do you play these instruments?

Key Words

Keyboard Family

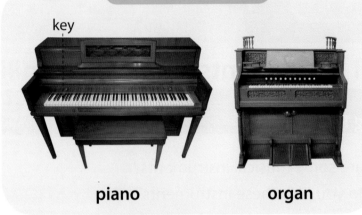

key

piano   organ

Woodwind Family

flute

clarinet

String Family

bow

violin   viola   cello

Brass Family

trumpet

trombone

Percussion Family

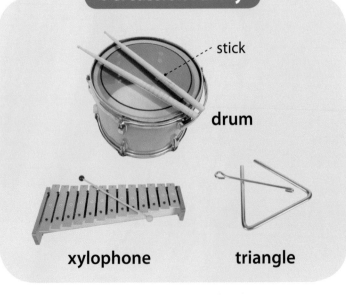

stick

drum

xylophone   triangle

Power Verbs

look alike
Some instruments **look alike**.

strike
Strike the piano keys.

belong to
The trumpet **belongs to** the brass family.

blow
Blow air into the flute.

Word Families : Tools for Musical Instruments

   **keyboard** ➡ A piano has a keyboard.

   **string** ➡ A violin has strings.

   **bow** ➡ You play the violin with a bow.

   **stick** ➡ You hit the drum with a stick.

Musical Instruments and Their Families

There are many musical instruments.
Some instruments look alike.
These instruments are in the same family.
Let's meet the instrument families.

Do you know any instruments with a keyboard?
The piano! That's right.
The piano has a keyboard.
The organ also has a keyboard.
They are in the keyboard family.
You strike the keys to play them.

piano   organ

Do you know any instruments with strings?
The violin? The cello? How about the viola?
They all belong to the string family.
You play them with a bow.

cello

violin   viola

The flute and clarinet belong to the woodwind family.
The trumpet and trombone belong to the brass family.
You blow air into them to play them.

I belong to the keyboard family.

I belong to the string family.

I belong to the woodwind family.

The drum, xylophone, and triangle belong to percussion family.
You hit them with a stick to play them.

I belong to the brass family.

I belong to the percussion family.

Check Understanding

1 **Which type of musical instrument does each picture show?**

a

b

_____   _____

2 **How do you play the trombone?**

a You strike the keys.   b You blow air into it.   c You hit it with a stick.

3 **What kind of instrument is the viola?**

a a woodwind   b a string instrument   c a brass instrument

4 **The _____ is a percussion instrument.**

a xylophone   b viola   c piano

- **Answer the questions below.**

1 What musical instruments have strings?

⇨ The _____, _____, and _____ have strings.

2 How do you play the cello?

⇨ You play the cello with a _____.

A **Look, Read, and Write.**
Look at the pictures. Write the correct words.

belongs to   blow   look alike   strike

1
_____ the piano keys.

2
_____ air into the clarinet.

3
The piano and organ
_____.

4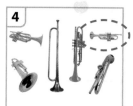
The trumpet
_____
the brass family.

B **Strings or Sticks?**
Draw a circle around the right words and then write the words.

1 The piano has a _____.
keyboard   string

2 The violin has _____.
strings   sticks

3 Play the violin with a _____.
stick   bow

4 Hit the drum with a _____.
stick   bow

A Look at the pictures. Write the correct words.

> built   blow   skip-count   mix

1 ▸ The third pig _____ a house with bricks.

2 12, 14, 16, 18, 20 ▸ Let's _____ by twos.

3 ⬤ + ⬤ = ⬤ ▸ _____ blue and red to make purple.

4 ▸ _____ air into the flute.

B Draw a circle around the right words and then write the words.

1 The big bad wolf _____ down the house. (blow)

    blowed   blew

2 Some people wear a pair of _____.

    glass   glasses

3 Cool colors make us feel _____.

    relaxed   relaxing

4 Play the cello with a _____.

    stick   bow

C Complete the sentences with the words below.

fell into	faster	come in	pairs
skip-counting	straw	sticks	bricks

1 The first little pig built a house with _____.

2 The second little pig built a house with _____.

3 The third little pig built a house with hard _____.

4 The big bad wolf _____ the boiling hot water.

5 Counting by twos is much _____ than counting by ones.

6 When we count by twos, we are "_____."

7 Many things come in groups of twos, or _____.

8 Shoes _____ pairs.

D Complete the sentences with the words below.

brass	keyboard	warm	woodwind
primary	mix	string	cool

1 There are three _____ colors.

2 We can _____ the primary colors together.

3 Red, yellow, and orange are _____ colors.

4 Blue, green, and purple are _____ colors.

5 The piano and organ are in the _____ family.

6 The violin and cello belong to the _____ family.

7 The flute and clarinet belong to the _____ family.

8 The trumpet and trombone belong to the _____ family.

Word List

Word List

01 Special Days
特別的日子

1	**special**	特別的	
2	**special day**	特別的日子	
3	**have a party**	舉辦派對	
4	**be coming**	將會前來	

*<be + V-ing>表即將發生

5	**will**	將……
6	**give**	給;送
7	**present**	禮物 (= gift)
8	**everyone**	每個人
9	**have**	吃 (= eat)
10	**cake**	蛋糕
11	**ice cream**	冰淇淋
12	**birthday**	生日
13	**celebrate**	慶祝
14	**every year**	每年
15	**family**	家庭 *複數: families
16	**with a cake**	用蛋糕

17	**Children's Day**	兒童節
18	**children**	兒童

*單數:child

19	**Mother's Day**	母親節

*Parents' Day:家長日

20	**mother**	母親
21	**Father's Day**	父親節
22	**father**	父親
23	**national holiday**	國定假日
24	**entire**	全部;整個
25	**Christmas**	聖誕節
26	**important**	重要的
27	**holiday**	節日;假日
28	**each other**	彼此
29	**gift**	禮物
30	**Thanksgiving**	感恩節
31	**another**	另一個
32	**American**	美國人
33	**share**	分享

34	special food	特別的食物
35	friend	朋友
36	also	也
37	honor	紀念
38	Independence Day	（美國）獨立紀念日
39	parade	遊行
40	firework(s)	煙火

02 The First Thanksgiving
感恩節的由來

1	the first	最早的
2	Thanksgiving	感恩節
3	America	美國
4	gather together	相聚
5	meal	膳食；一餐
6	be celebrated by	被……慶祝
7	the Pilgrims	清教徒前輩移民

*指西元1620年搭乘五月花號移居美國的英國清教徒
*pilgrim 朝聖者

8	group	群
9	for	為了……
10	religion	宗教
11	sail	航行
12	ship	船
13	called	名為
14	the *Mayflower*	《五月花號》
15	later	以後
16	finally	最後；終於
17	land in	登陸
18	snowy	下雪的

19	almost	幾乎
20	half of	半數的……
21	die	死亡 *過去式: died
22	during	在……期間
23	meet	遇見 *過去式: met
24	some	有些
25	Native American	美洲原住民
26	Squanto	斯夸托（人名）
27	stay with	與……待在一起
28	show	（透過示範）教導；演示
29	how to	如何
30	how to fish	如何捕魚
31	how to hunt	如何打獵
32	how to grow food	如何種植食物
33	lots of	很多……
34	food	食物
35	thank	感謝
36	big meal	大餐
37	invite	邀請
38	festival	節慶；慶典

03 What Is a Map?
什麼是地圖？

1	map	地圖
2	look at	看……
3	house	房屋
4	building	建築物
5	drawing	描繪；圖示
6	real	真實的

7	place	地方	36	now	現在
8	real place	實地	37	again	再一次
9	show	顯示	38	south of	……的南方
10	entire	全部	39	police station	警察局
11	the entire world	全世界	40	north of	……的北方
12	country	國家	41	fire station	消防局
13	city	城市	42	east of	……的東方
14	just	僅僅；只有	43	church	教堂
15	neighborhood	近鄰；鄰里	44	west of	……的西方

16 thing 物；東西

17 point to 指出……

18 school 學校

19 near 靠近……

20 sometimes 有時候

04 The Oceans and Continents
海洋和大陸

21 use 使用

22 direction 方位

23 find 找出

24 main 主要的

25 four (main) directions
四個（主要的）方位

1	ocean	海洋
2	continent	大陸
3	map of the world	世界地圖
4	be made up of	由……組成
5	body of land	陸地
6	body of water	水域
7	live on	居住在……
8	Asia	亞洲
9	largest	最大的

26 north 北方

27 south 南方

28 east 東方

29 west 西方

30 picture 圖片

*原級─比較級─最高級
large–larger–largest

31 like 像；如

32 letter 字母

33 if 如果

34 follow 跟隨

35 arrow 箭頭

10	Russia	俄羅斯
11	China	中國
12	Korea	韓國
13	Japan	日本
14	Europe	歐洲
15	be next to	鄰近……
16	England	英國

17	France	法國
18	Germany	德國
19	Africa	非洲
20	be near	靠近……
21	Egypt	埃及
22	South Africa	南非
23	be located in	位於……
24	North America	北美洲
25	South America	南美洲
26	be connected to	連接到……
27	each other	互相；彼此
28	the United States	美國
29	Canada	加拿大
30	Brazil	巴西
31	Argentina	阿根廷
32	Australia	澳洲
33	island	島
34	Antarctica	南極洲
35	at the bottom of	在……底端
36	be surrounded by	被……圍繞
37	Pacific Ocean	太平洋
38	biggest	最大的 *原級—比較級—最高級 big–bigger–biggest
39	on one side of	在……的一邊
40	on the other side of	在……的另一邊
41	Atlantic Ocean	大西洋
42	Indian Ocean	印度洋
43	Antarctic Ocean	南冰洋
44	Arctic Ocean	北冰洋

05 Where Do Plants Live?
植物生長在哪裡？

1	plant	植物
2	live in	住在；生活在
3	many places	許多地方
4	rainforest	雨林
5	wet	潮濕
6	get rain	下雨
7	tall	高大的
8	below	在……下面
9	ferns	蕨類植物
10	flowers	花朵
11	grow	生長；發育
12	forest floor	森林地表；森林植被
13	desert	沙漠
14	dry	乾燥
15	very little	很少
16	such	如此的；這樣的
17	desert plant	沙漠植物
18	thick	厚的；粗的
19	stem	莖
20	store	儲存
21	cactus	仙人掌
22	hold	保留
23	if	如果
24	rain	下雨
25	for a long time	很久；很長時間
26	even	甚至
27	tundra	凍原

28	snowy	下雪的
29	close together	緊靠；密集
30	survive	存活；活著

06 Amazing Plants
奇妙的植物

1	amazing	令人吃驚的；驚人的
2	more than	超過……
3	type	類型；種類
4	redwood (tree)	紅杉（樹）
5	tallest	最高的
		*原級─比較級─最高級
		tall–taller–tallest
6	in the world	世界上
7	grow in	生長於
8	California	（美國）加利福尼亞州
9	U.S.A.	美國
		(= United States of America)
10	100 meters	100公尺
11	rafflesia	大王花
12	jungle	叢林
13	one meter	1公尺
14	wide	寬的
		*原級─比較級─最高級
		wide–wider–widest
15	catch	捕捉
16	insect	昆蟲
17	insect-eating plant	食蟲植物
18	Venus flytrap	捕蠅草
19	hold	擁有
20	juice	汁；蜜露

21	land on	降落於……
22	quickly	迅速地
23	close	關閉
24	trap	誘捕
25	digest	消化
26	sundew plant	毛氈苔
27	be covered with	被……覆蓋
28	sticky	黏的
29	hair	毛
30	slowly	緩慢地
31	pitcher plant	豬籠草
32	look like	看起來像……
33	pitcher	水壺
34	splash	噗通一聲（狀聲詞）
35	fall into	掉進；落入
36	cup-shaped	杯狀的

07 What Lives in an Ocean?
海洋動物世界

1	ocean	海洋；洋
2	sea	海洋；海
3	fish	魚類
		*作魚的條數時單複數同形
4	crab	螃蟹
5	sea turtle	海龜
6	shark	鯊魚
7	dolphin	海豚
8	ocean animal	海洋動物
9	gills	鰓
10	breathe	呼吸

11	**fin**	鰭	
12	**tail**	尾	
13	**swim**	游泳	
14	**special**	特別的	
15	**take a look**	看一看；瞧一瞧	
16	**take a close look at**	仔細看看……	
17	**fast**	快；迅速	
18	**jaw**	下顎	
19	**sharp**	鋒利的；尖的	
20	**teeth**	牙齒 *tooth的複數	
21	**hunt**	獵取	
22	**well**	成功地；妥善地	
23	**blue water**	深海	
24	**sound**	聲音	
25	**far away**	遠處	
26	**from far away**	從遠處	
27	**nostril**	鼻孔	
28	**smell**	嗅聞	
29	**five hundred**	500	
30	**kind**	種類	
31	**dangerous**	危險的	
32	**great white shark**	大白鯊	
33	**the most dangerous**	最危險的	
34	**attack**	攻擊	
35	**anything**	任何事物	
36	**even**	甚至是……	

08 How Frogs Grow and Change
青蛙成長與變態過程

1	**frog**	青蛙
2	**grow**	生長；發育
3	**change**	變化
4	**ribbit**	呱呱（青蛙叫聲）
5	**pond**	池塘
6	**swamp**	沼澤
7	**lake**	湖泊
8	**land**	陸地
9	**both**	兩者（都）
10	**on land**	在陸地上
11	**in the water**	在水裡
12	**front leg**	前腿
13	**back leg**	後腿
14	**leap**	跳躍
15	**webbed**	有蹼的
16	**webbed feet**	蹼足
17	**wet**	潮濕的
18	**smooth**	光滑的
19	**skin**	皮膚
20	**catch**	捕捉
21	**bug**	蟲子
22	**tongue**	舌頭
23	**always**	一直
24	**look like**	看起來像……
25	**baby**	嬰兒 *複數: babies
26	**look different**	看起來不同

27	tadpole	蝌蚪	
28	baby frog	幼蛙	
29	lay eggs	產卵	
30	hatch	孵出	
31	only	僅僅；只	
32	tail	尾巴	
33	gradually	漸漸地	
34	develop	發展	
35	disappear	消失	
36	a few weeks	數週	
37	become	變成	
38	adult frog	成蛙	

09 The Three Little Pigs
三隻小豬的故事

1	little pig	小豬
2	once upon a time	很久很久以前
3	one day	有一天
4	decide to	決定去……
5	own	自己的
6	the first	第一個
7	build	建造 *過去式: built
8	straw	稻草
9	with straw	用稻草
10	the second	第二個
11	stick	樹枝
12	the third	第三個
13	hard	堅硬的
14	brick	磚頭

15	woods	樹林；森林
16	bad	壞的
17	wolf	狼
18	house of straw	稻草屋
19	yum	好吃
20	yummy	好吃的；美味的
21	think	想 *過去式: thought
22	soon	不久；很快地
23	come up to	來到……
24	knock	敲
25	let	允許；讓
26	answer	回答
27	Not by the hair of my chinny chin chin	我對下巴上的鬍子發誓「不行！」
28	huff	吹氣
29	puff	一陣陣地吹
30	blow down	吹倒 *過去式: blew down
31	run away	逃跑 *過去式: ran away
32	the second pig's house	第二隻小豬的房子
33	house of sticks	木屋
34	the third little pig's house	第三隻小豬的房子
35	the house of bricks	磚瓦屋
36	too . . . to . . .	太……以致不能……
37	strong	堅固的
38	chimney	煙囪
39	climb up	爬上
40	roof	屋頂

41	get into	進入……
42	through	從……；經由……
43	himself	他自己
44	jump down	跳下
45	clever	聰明的
46	pot	鍋
47	boiling water	沸騰的水
48	fireplace	壁爐
49	splash	噗通一聲（狀聲詞）
50	fall into	掉進
		*過去式: fell into
51	scream	尖叫
52	yell	吼叫
53	happily	快樂地
54	ever after	從此以後一直

10 Skip-Counting
跳數

1	counting	計算；數
2	skip-counting	跳數
3	count	計算；數
4	one by one	一個一個地
5	by twos	兩個兩個地
6	much faster than	比……快很多
7	by ones	一個一個地
8	skip-count	跳數
9	shoes	鞋子
10	find out	找出
11	be grouped	被分組

12	pair	一對；一雙
13	twelve	12；十二
14	six pairs	六對；六雙
15	come in	有
16	a pair of eyes	一對眼睛
17	a pair of arms	一雙手臂
18	a pair of legs	一雙腿
19	wear	穿；戴
20	a pair of socks	一雙襪子
21	a pair of gloves	一雙手套
22	a pair of glasses	一副眼鏡

11 Colors
色彩的奧妙

1	look around	環顧四周
2	blue sky	藍天
3	green grass	綠草
4	a bunch of	一串……
5	color	顏色
6	everywhere	到處
7	name	列舉
8	primary color	原色
9	red	紅色
10	yellow	黃色
11	blue	藍色
12	mix	混合
13	green	綠色
14	purple	紫色
15	orange	橘色

16	combine	結合
17	black	黑色
17	warm color	暖色
19	make	獲得
20	feel excited	感到興奮
21	cool color	冷色
22	feel relaxed	感到放鬆
23	exciting	令人興奮的
24	calm	平靜

12 Musical Instruments and Their Families
樂器和樂器家族

1	musical instrument	樂器
2	family	家族
3	look alike	看起來很像
4	the same	相同；很像
5	keyboard	鍵盤
6	organ	風琴
7	keyboard family	鍵盤樂器家族
8	play	演奏
9	strike	敲
10	key	鍵
11	string	弦
12	violin	小提琴
13	cello	大提琴
14	viola	中提琴
15	belong to	屬於……
16	string family	弦樂器家族

17	bow	弓
18	flute	長笛
19	clarinet	豎笛
20	woodwind family	木管樂器家族
21	blow	吹
22	blow air into	把空氣吹進……
23	trumpet	喇叭
24	trombone	長號
25	brass family	銅管樂器家族
26	xylophone	木琴
27	triangle	三角鐵
28	percussion family	打擊樂器家族
29	hit	打；打擊
30	stick	棒子

Answers and Translations

Unit 01 Special Days
特別的日子

Reading Focus 閱讀焦點

• What are some special days? 有哪些特別的日子？

• Why do we celebrate special days? 為什麼要慶祝這些特別的日子？

• What special things do we do on special days? 在特別的日子裡，我們會做哪些特別的事？

Key Words 關鍵字彙

birthday 生日

Children's Day 兒童節

Families' Special Days 家庭的特別日子

Mother's Day 母親節

Father's Day 父親節

Christmas 聖誕節

Thanksgiving 感恩節

Holidays 節日

New Year's Day 新年

Independence Day （美國）獨立紀念日

Power Verbs 核心動詞

have a party 舉辦派對
Let's **have a** birthday **party**.
讓我們舉辦一個生日派對吧。

celebrate 慶祝
We **celebrate** Christmas.
我們慶祝聖誕節。

share 分享
We **share** special food.
我們分享特別的食物。

honor 紀念
Americans **honor** Independence Day.
美國人紀念獨立紀念日。

Word Families : Special Days
相關字彙：特別的日子

birthday 生日
→ **cake** 蛋糕
candle 蠟燭
present 禮物

Christmas 聖誕節
→ **gift** 禮物
Christmas tree 聖誕樹
Santa Claus 聖誕老人

Independence Day （美國）獨立紀念日
→ **parade** 遊行
fireworks 煙火
picnic 野餐

Special Days 特別的日子

提姆今天將舉辦一個生日派對，
他的朋友會到他家，
他們會送他禮物，
每個人都會吃蛋糕和冰淇淋。
這天是什麼特別的日子？
這天是提姆的生日。

有許多特別的日子，
我們每年都會慶祝這些特別的日子。

許多家庭會準備蛋糕來慶祝生日。
兒童節是屬於兒童的特別日子；
母親節是屬於母親的特別日子；
父親節是屬於父親的特別日子。

也有許多國定假日。
全國上下都會慶祝這些國定假日。

聖誕節是重要的節日，
人們在那天會互送禮物。

感恩節是另一個大節，
美國人會和他們的家人、朋友分享特別的食物。

美國人也會紀念獨立紀念日，
他們會舉辦遊行和施放煙火，來慶祝國家的生日。

Check Understanding 文意測驗

1 下列圖片各代表哪個特別的日子？
   a **Christmas** 聖誕節   **b** **birthday** 生日

2 許多家庭會準備_____來慶祝生日   **a**
   a 蛋糕   **b** 禮物   **c** 冰淇淋

3 我們多久慶祝一次節日？ **c**
   a 每天   **b** 每月   **c** 每年

4 _____是屬於母親的特別日子。 **a**
   a 母親節   **b** 父親節   **c** 兒童節

● 回答問題

1 What is a special day for children? 哪個節日是屬於兒童的特別日子？
   ⇨ **Children's** **Day** is a special day for children. 兒童節是屬於兒童的特別日子。

2 How do Americans celebrate Independence Day? 美國人如何慶祝獨立紀念日？
   ⇨ They celebrate it with **parades** and **fireworks**. 他們會舉辦遊行和施放煙火，來慶祝這個節日。

Vocabulary and Grammar Builder 字彙與文法練習

A 看圖填空：依照圖片選出正確的單字。

1 People **celebrate** birthdays with cakes. 人們用蛋糕慶祝生日。

2 Americans share special foods on **Thanksgiving**. 美國人在感恩節會分享特別的食物。

3 Americans **honor** Independence Day. 美國人紀念獨立紀念日。

4 People give each other **gifts** on Christmas. 人們在聖誕節會給彼此禮物。

B 現在式Have還是進行式Having？圈出正確的單字，並填入空格中。

1 Tim is ___**having**___ a party today. 今天提姆將舉辦生日派對。
   have (having)

2 His friends are ___**coming**___ to his house. 他的朋友會來他的家裡。
   come (coming)

3 They will ___**give**___ him presents. 他們會送他禮物。
   (give) giving

4 Everyone will ___**have**___ cake and ice cream. 每個人都會吃蛋糕和冰淇淋。
   (have) having

Unit 02

The First Thanksgiving

最早的感恩節由來

Reading Focus 閱讀焦點

- When was the first Thanksgiving? 最早的感恩節始於何時？
- Who were the Pilgrims? 誰是清教徒前輩移民？
- Who helped the Pilgrims? 誰幫助了清教徒前輩移民？

Key Words 關鍵字彙

Pilgrims 清教徒前輩移民

religion 宗教信仰

The First Thanksgiving 最早的感恩節

Mayflower 《五月花號》

Native American 美洲原住民

festival 節日

Thanksgiving Foods 感恩節食物

turkey 火雞

pumpkin pie 南瓜派

Power Verbs 核心動詞

gather together 相聚
Families **gather together** on Thanksgiving.
在感恩節那天家人會團聚。

sail 航行
The Pilgrims **sailed** to America.
清教徒前輩移民航行到美洲。

land in 登陸
The Pilgrims **landed in** America.
清教徒前輩移民在美洲登陸。

die 死亡
Many people **died** during the winter.
許多人在這個冬天喪生。

stay with 與……待在一起
He **stayed with** the Pilgrims.
他與清教徒前輩移民們待在一起。

thank 感謝
They **thanked** God.
他們感謝上帝。

Word Families : Actions 相關字彙：動作

fish 捕魚
how to fish 如何捕魚

hunt 打獵
how to hunt 如何打獵

how to 如何

grow food 種植食物
how to grow food 如何種植食物

speak English 說英文
how to speak English 如何說英文

The First Thanksgiving 最早的感恩節由來

感恩節在美國是大節日，
在這天家人會團聚，並享用特別的餐點。

最早的感恩節慶祝活動，始於清教徒前輩移民。
這群清教徒前輩移民來自英國，
他們為了宗教信仰而到美國。

清教徒前輩移民搭乘一艘名叫《五月花號》的帆船，
兩個月後，他們終於在美洲登陸。
當時是西元1620年的冬天。

這個冬天非常冷又下雪，
幾乎半數的清教徒前輩移民，都在這個冬天喪生。

到了春天，他們遇見一些美洲原住民，
他們對清教徒前輩移民伸出援手，

其中一個叫斯夸托的美洲原住民會講英語，
他留在清教徒前輩移民身邊幫助他們。
他教他們如何捕魚；
他教他們如何打獵；
他教他們如何栽種食物。

那年秋天，清教徒前輩移民擁有許多食物。
他們感謝上帝，
他們也感謝美洲原住民們。
於是他們準備了豐富的佳餚，
邀請美洲原住民們來享用，
他們連續三天舉行了盛大的節慶，
那就是感恩節的由來。

Check Understanding 文意測驗

1 下列圖片各代表哪個事件？將答案填入空格。

   a The **Pilgrims** went to America. 這些清教徒前輩移民去美國。

   b They met the **Native Americans**. 他們遇見美洲原住民。

2 清教徒前輩移民移民自_____。 **b**

   a 美國   b 英國   c 加拿大

3 誰是斯夸托？ **c**

   a 清教徒前輩移民   b 漁夫   c 美洲原住民

4 為什麼清教徒前輩移民，要邀請美洲原住民共享佳餚？ **c**

   a 為了捕魚   b 為了種植食物   c 為了感謝他們

● 回答問題

1 How did the Pilgrims go to America? 清教徒前輩移民是如何去美洲的？
   ⇨ They sailed on the *Mayflower*. 他們搭乘《五月花號》。

2 How did Squanto help the Pilgrims? 斯夸托如何幫助清教徒前輩移民？
   ⇨ He showed them how to **fish**, **hunt**, and **grow** food.
      他教他們如何捕魚、打獵和種植食物。

Vocabulary and Grammar Builder 字彙與文法練習

Ⓐ 看圖填空：依照圖片選出正確的單字。

   1 The Pilgrims sailed on the *Mayflower*. 這些清教徒前輩移民們搭乘《五月花號》。

   2 The Pilgrims went to America for their **religion**. 清教徒前輩移民為了宗教信仰而到美國。

   3 The **Native Americans** helped the Pilgrims. 美洲原住民幫助這些清教徒前輩移民。

   4 They had a **big meal**. 他們享用了一頓豐盛的佳餚。

Ⓑ 是Sailed（航行）還是Landed（登陸）？圈出正確的單字，並填入空格中。

   1 The Pilgrims ____**landed**____ in America. 清教徒前輩移民在美洲登陸。
      sailed (landed)

   2 Squanto ____**stayed**____ with the Pilgrims. 斯夸托與這些清教徒前輩移民待在一起。
      showed (stayed)

   3 The Pilgrims ____**thanked**____ the Native Americans. 清教徒前輩移民感謝這些美洲原住民們。
      (thanked) sailed

   4 The Pilgrims ____**invited**____ the Native Americans. 清教徒前輩移民邀請這些美洲原住民們。
      stayed (invited)

What Is a Map?

什麼是地圖？

Reading Focus 閱讀焦點

- What is a map? 什麼是地圖？
- Why do people use maps? 為什麼人們要使用地圖？
- What are the four main directions? 四個主要的方位是什麼？

Key Words 關鍵字彙

Maps 地圖

world map
世界地圖

country map
國家地圖

city map
城市地圖

neighborhood map
鄰里地圖

Power Verbs 核心動詞

show
顯示

A map **shows** many places.
地圖能顯示許多地方。

point
指出

Point to the school on the map.
在地圖上指出學校。

find
找出

Can you **find** the school?
你能找出學校嗎？

follow
跟隨

Just **follow** the arrow.
只要跟著箭頭走。

Directions 方位

North
北方

West
西方

East
東方

South
南方

N 北方
W 西方 E 東方
S 南方

Word Families : Places 相關字彙：地點

Our World 我們的世界

world
世界

country
國家

city
城市

my house
我的家

neighborhood
鄰里地區

What Is a Map? 什麼是地圖？

看著地圖，
你可以看到許多房屋、樹木和建築物。

地圖是實地的圖示，
地圖能顯示許多地方。
它能呈現全世界；
它能呈現一個國家，或是一個城市；
它也能只呈現一個小鄰里。

地圖幫助你瞭解事物的地點，
在地圖上指出學校的位置，
學校在哪裡？
學校在房子的旁邊。

有時候我們會用方位來找一個地點。

有四個主要的方位，
分別是北方、南方、東方和西方。

許多地圖會使用像這樣的圖示，
N、S、E 和 W 這些字母，代表：
「北方」、「南方」、「東方」和「西方」。
如果跟著箭頭方向走，你就能朝著那個方向前進。

現在，再看一次地圖，
學校在哪裡？
學校在房子的南邊，
警察局在房子的北邊，
消防局在房子的東邊，
教堂在房子的西邊。

Check Understanding 文意測驗

1 以下圖片屬於哪種地圖？

 a a map of the <u>world</u> 世界地圖 b a map of a <u>neighborhood</u> 鄰里地圖

2 _____幫助你瞭解事物的位置。 **b**

 a 建築物 b 地圖 c 公園

3 有時候，我們會用_____來找一個地點。 **c**

 a 樹 b 圖畫 c 方位

4 東方和西方是？ **a**

 a 方位 b 地點 c 地圖

● 回答問題

1 What are the four main directions? 四個主要的方位是什麼？
 ⇨ They are <u>north</u>, <u>south</u>, <u>east</u>, and <u>west</u>. 北方、南方、東方和西方。

2 What can a map show? 地圖能顯示什麼？
 ⇨ It can show the entire <u>world</u> or just a small <u>neighborhood</u>.
   它能呈現全世界或僅一個小鄰里。

Vocabulary and Grammar Builder 字彙與文法練習

Ⓐ 看圖填空：依照圖片選出正確的單字。

 1 A map can <u>show</u> many places. 地圖能顯示許多地點。

 2 <u>Point</u> to the fire station on the map. 在地圖上指出消防局。

 3 Just <u>follow</u> the arrow. 跟著箭頭走。

 4 We use directions to <u>find</u> a place. 我們使用方位來找地方。

Ⓑ 北方或南方？圈出正確的單字，並填入空格中。

 1 The police station is ___**north**___ of the house. 警察局在房子的北方。
  south (north)

 2 The school is ___**south**___ of the house. 學校在房子的南方。
  (south) north

 3 The church is ___**west**___ of the house. 教堂在房子的西方。
  east (west)

 4 The fire station is ___**east**___ of the house. 消防局在房子的東方。
  (east) west

Unit 04 The Oceans and Continents
海洋和大陸

Reading Focus 閱讀焦點

- What is a continent? 什麼是大陸？
- What is an ocean? 什麼是海洋？
- What continent do you live on? 你居住在哪個大陸？

Key Words 關鍵字彙

Seven Continents
七塊大陸

Europe 歐洲
Asia 亞洲
North America 北美洲
Africa 非洲
Australia 澳洲
South America 南美洲
Antarctica 南極洲

Five Oceans
五個海洋

Arctic Ocean 北冰洋
Atlantic Ocean 大西洋
Pacific Ocean 太平洋
Indian Ocean 印度洋
Antarctic Ocean 南冰洋

Power Verbs 核心動詞

be made up of
由……組成

Earth is made up of continents and oceans.
地球由大陸和海洋組成。

be located in
位於

Korea is located in Asia.
韓國位於亞洲。

be connected to
連接

China is connected to Russia.
中國和俄羅斯連接在一起。

be surrounded by
圍繞

An island is surrounded by water.
島的四周被水圍繞。

Word Families : Positions 相關字彙：位置

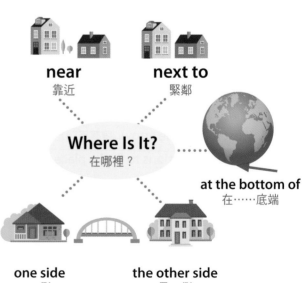

near 靠近

next to 緊鄰

Where Is It? 在哪裡？

at the bottom of 在……底端

one side 一側

the other side 另一側

110

The Oceans and Continents 海洋和大陸

看看世界地圖，
地球是由大陸和海洋組成。

大陸是體積非常大的陸地，
地球上有七個大陸；
海洋是體積非常大的水域，
地球上有五個大洋。

我們居住在大陸上，
亞洲是最大的大陸，
俄羅斯、中國、韓國和日本都在亞洲。.

歐洲鄰近亞洲，
英國、法國和德國都在歐洲。

非洲鄰近歐洲和亞洲，
埃及和南非都位於非洲。

北美洲和南美洲互相連接，
美國和加拿大都位於北美洲；
巴西和阿根廷都位於南美洲。

澳洲是一座大陸島，
南極洲在地球的底端。

大陸被海洋環繞，
太平洋是世界最大的海洋，
亞洲在它旁邊；
北美洲和南美洲在另一邊。

Check Understanding 文意測驗

1 以下圖片各顯示哪個大陸？
   a Africa 非洲
   b Australia 澳洲

2 什麼是大陸？ **a**
   a 體積大的陸地
   b 體積大的海洋
   c 體積大的水域

3 哪個國家在非洲？ **c**
   a 韓國
   b 英國
   c 埃及

4 南極洲在地球的_____。 **c**
   a 上方
   b 側邊
   c 底端

● 回答問題

1 What two things is Earth made up of? 地球由哪兩種東西組成？
   ⇨ Earth is made up of <u>continents</u> and <u>oceans</u>. 地球由大陸和海洋組成。

2 Name the seven continents on Earth. 列出地球上的七個大陸。
   ⇨ They are <u>Asia</u>, <u>Europe</u>, Africa, <u>North America</u>, South America, Australia, and <u>Antarctica</u>.
   亞洲、歐洲、非洲、北美洲、南美洲、澳洲和南極洲。

Vocabulary and Grammar Builder 字彙與文法練習

Ⓐ 看圖填空：依照圖片選出正確的單字。

1 The <u>Pacific Ocean</u> is the biggest ocean. 太平洋是最大的海洋。

2 Korea and Japan are located in <u>Asia</u>. 韓國和日本位於亞洲。

3 Brazil and Argentina are in <u>South America</u>. 巴西和阿根廷在南美洲。

4 Australia is an <u>island</u> continent. 澳洲是一座大陸島。

Ⓑ Next（靠近）或Next to（緊鄰）？圈出正確的單字，並填入空格中。

1 Europe is ___**next to**___ Asia. 歐洲緊鄰著亞洲。
   next (next to)

2 The continents are ___**surrounded by**___ water. 大陸被水域環繞。
   surround (surrounded by)

3 The United States is ___**located in**___ North America. 美國位於北美洲。
   locate (located in)

4 North and South America are ___**connected to**___ each other. 北美洲和南美洲互相連接。
   connect (connected to)

111

Where Do Plants Live?

植物生長在哪裡？

Reading Focus 閱讀焦點

- What kinds of plants grow in rainforests? 哪些植物生長在雨林裡？
- What kinds of plants grow in deserts? 哪些植物生長在沙漠裡？
- What kinds of plants grow in tundra? 哪些植物生長在凍原裡？

Key Words 關鍵字彙

Places to Live 居住環境

forest 森林

rainforest 雨林

desert 沙漠

tundra 凍原

grassland 草原

Types of Plants 植物的種類

oak tree 橡樹

maple tree 楓樹

fern 蕨類植物

cactus 仙人掌

wildflower 野花

Power Verbs 核心動詞

get rain 降雨

Rainforests **get** lots of **rain**.
雨林的降雨量非常多。

store 儲存

Desert plants **store** water.
沙漠植物會儲存水分。

hold 保留

Plants' roots **hold** water.
植物的根會保留水分。

survive 存活

Plants can **survive** in the cold.
植物能在寒冷中存活。

Word Families : Living Places
相關字彙：生長環境

 rainforest 雨林 ⟹ hot and wet 炎熱潮濕

 **desert** 沙漠 ⟹ hot and dry 炎熱乾燥

 tundra 凍原 ⟹ cold and snowy 寒冷有雪

 grassland 草原 ⟹ covered with grass 布滿草

Where Do Plants Live? 植物生長在哪裡？

植物生長在許多地方。

許多植物生長在雨林裡，
雨林是炎熱潮溼的地方，
它的雨量非常多。

雨林裡有許多高大的樹木，
它們通常擁有大片的樹葉，
在高大的樹木底下，有許多較矮小的植物。
蕨類植物和花朵，生長在森林地表。

有些植物生長在沙漠，
沙漠是炎熱乾燥的地方，
它的雨量非常稀少，
植物是如何在這麼炎熱乾燥的地方生長的？

許多沙漠植物有很肥厚的莖，
可以幫助植物儲存水分。
仙人掌是沙漠植物，
它可以將水分保留在肥厚的莖裡，
如果很久沒降雨，
就可以在之後利用這些水分。

有些植物甚至生存在凍原，
凍原是寒冷有雪的地方，
凍原植物非常矮小，
它們緊鄰著生長，
這樣能幫助它們在寒冷的凍原存活。

Check Understanding 文意測驗

1 以下圖片是什麼地方？
  a **desert** 沙漠　　　　　　　　b **rainforest** 雨林

2 哪個地方雨量很少？ **b**
  a 雨林　　　　　b 沙漠　　　　　c 凍原

3 凍原的天氣型態是什麼？ **c**
  a 寒冷乾燥　　　　b 炎熱潮濕　　　　c 寒冷有雪

4 仙人掌將水分保留在肥厚的_____內。 **b**
  a 根　　　　　b 莖　　　　　c 葉片

● 回答問題

1 What do the trees in rainforests look like? 雨林裡的樹木外觀如何？
  ⇨ They are <u>tall</u> and have <u>large</u> leaves. 它們長得高大且有大片的樹葉。

2 How can plants grow in a hot and dry desert? 植物如何在炎熱乾燥的沙漠生長？
  ⇨ They can store <u>water</u> in their <u>thick stems</u>. 它們能將水分儲存於肥厚的莖內。

Vocabulary and Grammar Builder 字彙與文法練習

Ⓐ 看圖填空：依照圖片選出正確的單字。

  1 <u>Rainforests</u> get lots of rain. 雨林的雨量很多。

  2 <u>Deserts</u> get very little rain. 沙漠的雨量很少。

  3 <u>Ferns</u> grow on the forest floor. 蕨類植物生長於地表。

  4 Plants in the <u>tundra</u> are not tall. 凍原植物並不高大。

Ⓑ Dry（乾燥）或Wet（潮濕）？圈出正確的單字，並填入空格中。

  1 A rainforest is a hot, ___wet___ place. 雨林是炎熱潮溼的地方。
    dry (wet)

  2 Plants in rainforests have ___large___ leaves. 雨林植物有大葉片。
    small (large)

  3 The stem of a cactus is ___thick___ . 仙人掌的莖肥厚。
    (thick) thin

  4 Tundra is a cold, ___snowy___ place. 凍原是寒冷有雪的地方。
    sunny (snowy)

Unit 06 — Amazing Plants
奇妙的植物

Reading Focus 閱讀焦點

- What is the world's tallest plant? 世界上最高的植物是什麼？
- What is the world's biggest flower? 世界上最大的花是哪種花？
- What are some insect-eating plants? 哪些植物是食蟲植物？

Key Words 關鍵字彙

Amazing Plants
奇妙的植物

redwood tree
紅杉樹
the world's tallest tree
世界上最高的樹

rafflesia
大王花
the world's biggest flower
世界上最大的花

Insect-Eating Plants
食蟲植物

Venus flytrap 捕蠅草　**sundew plant** 毛氈苔　**pitcher plant** 豬籠草

long spine
長長的刺毛

sticky hairs
可分泌黏液的毛

cup-shaped leaf
瓶狀葉片

Power Verbs 核心動詞

catch 捕捉　　**land on** 降落於……　　**trap** 誘捕

Some plants **catch** insects.
有些植物會捕捉昆蟲。

Insects **land on** the leaf.
昆蟲降落於葉片上。

The leaf **traps** the insect.
葉片會誘捕昆蟲。

be covered with 被……覆蓋　　**look like** 看起來像……　　**fall into** 掉進

The leaf is **covered with** hairs.
葉片被絨毛覆蓋。

The leaf **looks like** a pitcher.
葉片看起來像水壺。

Insects **fall into** the hole.
昆蟲掉進洞裡。

Word Families 相關字彙

amazing 令人驚嘆的　　**tall** 高大的　　**wide** 寬的

sticky 黏的　　**cup-shaped** 杯狀的　　**pitcher** 水壺

Amazing Plants 奇妙的植物

世界上有超過300,000種植物，
有些植物非常奇妙。

紅杉樹是世界最高的樹種，
生長於美國加州，
有些紅杉樹可長到超過100公尺。

大王花是世界上最大的花，
生長於亞洲的叢林，
這種花可寬達一公尺。

有些植物會捕捉昆蟲，
它們屬於食蟲植物。

捕蠅草有著特殊的葉片，
這些葉片會分泌蜜露。

當昆蟲停靠在上面，
葉片就會迅速地關閉，
這些葉片誘捕昆蟲，
再由捕蠅草的消化液將其消化。

毛氈苔也有特殊的葉片，
這些葉片由可分泌黏液的毛覆蓋，
當昆蟲停留在黏毛上，
葉片就會緩慢地關閉，
再由毛氈苔的消化液將其消化。

豬籠草擁有看似水壺的葉片，
當昆蟲「噗通」一聲掉落到杯狀葉片裡，
豬籠草的消化液就會將其消化。

Check Understanding 文意測驗

1 以下圖片是哪種植物？
   a sundew plant 毛氈苔   **b** redwood (tree) 紅杉樹

2 哪種植物可以長到超過一公尺寬？ **c**
   a 紅杉樹   **b** 豬籠草   **c** 大王花

3 哪種植物可以捕捉昆蟲？ **c**
   a 大王花   **b** 紅杉樹   **c** 捕蠅草

4 毛氈苔的葉片有許多_____毛。 **b**
   a 多汁的   **b** 可分泌黏液的   **c** 大的

● 回答問題

1 What is the world's tallest tree? 世界上最高的樹是哪種樹？
   ⇨The redwood tree is the tallest tree in the world. 紅杉樹是世界上最高的樹。

2 What are some insect-eating plants? 哪些植物是食蟲植物？
   ⇨ They are the Venus flytrap, sundew plant, and pitcher plant.
      捕蠅草、毛氈苔和豬籠草。

Vocabulary and Grammar Builder 字彙與文法練習

Ⓐ 看圖填空：依照圖片選出正確的單字。

1 The leaves of a Venus flytrap trap insects. 捕蠅草的葉片會誘捕昆蟲。

2 Insects land on the sticky hairs. 昆蟲停靠在黏毛上。

3 Insects fall into the cup-shaped leaf. 昆蟲掉進杯狀葉片裡。

4 Juices from the plant digest the insect. 植物分泌的蜜露把昆蟲消化。

Ⓑ Wide（寬闊的）或Tall（高大的）？圈出正確的單字，並填入空格中。

1 Insect-eating plants are ____amazing____ . 食蟲植物令人驚嘆。
   amaze (amazing)

2 The redwood tree can grow more than 100 meters ____tall____ . 紅杉樹可長到高達一百公尺。
   (tall) wide

3 The rafflesia is the ____biggest____ flower in the world. 大王花是世界上最大的花。
   big (biggest)

4 The pitcher plant has ____cup-shaped____ leaves. 豬籠草有杯狀葉片。
   (cup-shaped) cup-shape

115

Unit 07

What Lives in an Ocean?
海洋動物世界

Reading Focus 閱讀焦點

- What are some ocean animals? 海洋動物有哪些？
- How are these ocean animals alike? 這些海洋動物有什麼共同點？
- How are sharks special? 鯊魚有什麼特別？

Key Words 關鍵字彙

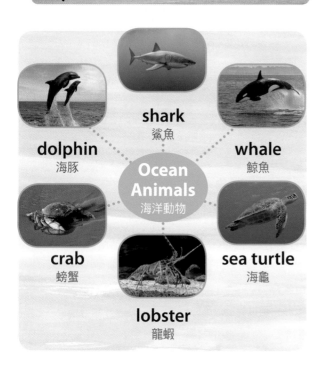

dolphin 海豚
shark 鯊魚
whale 鯨魚
crab 螃蟹
Ocean Animals 海洋動物
sea turtle 海龜
lobster 龍蝦

Power Verbs 核心動詞

breathe 呼吸

Fish **breathe** in water.
魚在水裡呼吸。

take a close look at 仔細瞧瞧

Let's **take a close look at** a shark.
讓我們仔細瞧瞧鯊魚吧。

hunt 獵食

Sharks **hunt** fish.
鯊魚獵食魚類。

attack 攻擊

Great white sharks **attack** people.
大白鯊會攻擊人類。

A Shark's Body Parts
鯊魚的身體部位

eyes 眼睛
gill slits 鰓裂
skin 皮膚
tail 尾
nostrils 鼻孔
jaws 下顎
fins 鰭

Word Families : A Shark's Body Parts
相關字彙：鯊魚的身體部位

Sharks are special. 鯊魚很特別。

fins 鰭 ⇒ Sharks have large and long fins.
鯊魚有大且長的鰭。

tail 尾巴 ⇒ Some sharks have a very long tail.
有些鯊魚有非常長的尾巴。

jaws 下顎 ⇒ Sharks' jaws have many sharp teeth.
鯊魚的下顎有許多尖利的牙齒。

nostrils 鼻孔 ⇒ Sharks use their nostrils to smell.
鯊魚用鼻孔嗅聞。

What Lives in an Ocean? 海洋動物世界

大洋是面積很大的海，
許多植物和動物都居住在大洋裡，
魚類、蟹類、海龜、鯊魚和海豚，都是海洋動物。

所有魚類都住在水裡且有鰓。
魚鰓幫助魚類在水裡呼吸。

魚類也有鰭和尾，
牠們用鰭和尾游泳。

看看這些鯊魚們！
牠們是魚類嗎？
是的，鯊魚是魚類，但牠們很特別。
讓我們仔細瞧瞧鯊魚吧！

鯊魚有大且長的鰭，
這些鰭和尾幫助鯊魚游得快。

鯊魚有很大的下顎和尖利的牙齒，
鯊魚的牙齒幫助牠們獵食魚類。

鯊魚能在海洋裡看得很清楚，
鯊魚能聽見遠處的聲音，
鯊魚用鼻孔嗅聞。

世界上有超過五百種鯊魚，
有些鯊魚非常危險，
大白鯊是最危險的鯊魚種類，
牠會攻擊所有物體——連人類也無法倖免！

Check Understanding 文意測驗

1 以下圖片是哪種動物？
   a shark 鯊魚   **b** sea turtle 海龜

2 所有的魚類都有什麼？ **b**
   a 大的尾巴   **b** 魚鰓   **c** 尖利的牙齒

3 什麼東西能幫助鯊魚游得很快？ **c**
   a 鰓和尾巴   **b** 鰭和牙齒   **c** 鰭和尾巴

4 鯊魚用_____嗅聞。 **c**
   a 鰭   **b** 下顎   **c** 鼻孔

● 回答問題

1 What are some ocean animals? 海洋動物有哪些？
   ⇨ They are <u>fish</u>, <u>crabs</u>, <u>sea turtles</u>, sharks, and <u>dolphins</u>. 魚類、螃蟹、海龜、鯊魚和海豚。

2 Which shark is the most dangerous? 哪種鯊魚最危險？
   ⇨ The <u>great</u> <u>white</u> <u>shark</u> is the most dangerous shark. 大白鯊是最危險的鯊魚種類。

Vocabulary and Grammar Builder 字彙與文法練習

Ⓐ 看圖填空：依照圖片選出正確的單字。

1 <u>Gills</u> help fish breathe in water. 魚鰓幫助魚類在水裡呼吸。

2 Fish use their <u>fins</u> to swim. 魚類用牠們的鰭來游泳。

3 Sharks <u>hunt</u> other ocean animals. 鯊魚會獵食其他的海洋動物。

4 The great white shark can <u>attack</u> people. 大白鯊會攻擊人類。

Ⓑ 這是哪個部位？圈出正確的單字，並填入空格中。

1 Sharks have large ____jaws____. 鯊魚有很大的下顎。
   nostrils (jaws)

2 Sharks' large and long ____fins____ help them swim fast. 鯊魚的長鰭幫助牠們游得快。
   gills (fins)

3 Sharks' sharp ____teeth____ help them hunt well. 鯊魚的尖牙幫助牠們獵食。
   mouth (teeth)

4 Sharks use their ____nostrils____ to smell. 鯊魚用牠們的鼻孔嗅聞。
   (nostrils) gills

Unit 08
How Frogs Grow and Change
青蛙成長與變態過程

Reading Focus 閱讀焦點
- Where do frogs live? 青蛙生活在哪裡？
- What is a tadpole? 蝌蚪是什麼？
- How does a frog grow? 青蛙是如何生長發育的？

Key Words 關鍵字彙

frog 青蛙   **tadpole** 蝌蚪   **frog eggs** 青蛙卵

A Frog's Body Parts
青蛙的身體部位

skin 皮膚
eyes 眼睛
back legs 後腿
tongue 舌頭
front legs 前腿
webbed feet 蹼足

Power Verbs 核心動詞

 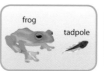

leap 跳躍
Frogs can **leap** high.
青蛙能跳得很高。

look different 看起來不同
Frogs and tadpoles **look different**.
青蛙和蝌蚪看起來不同。

lay eggs 產卵
Frogs **lay eggs**.
青蛙產卵。

hatch 孵出
Tadpoles **hatch** from eggs.
蝌蚪由卵中孵出。

develop 發育
Tadpoles **develop** legs.
蝌蚪發育出腿部。

disappear 消失
Tadpoles' tails **disappear**.
蝌蚪的尾巴消失。

Word Families : A Frog's Habitats
相關字彙：青蛙的生長環境

pond 池塘   **swamp** 沼澤

Where Frogs Live 青蛙的生長環境

lake 湖泊   **land** 陸地

How Frogs Grow and Change 青蛙成長與變態過程

呱呱，呱呱，呱呱。
你有聽到蛙鳴聲嗎？

青蛙生活在許多地點，
牠們生活於池塘、沼澤和湖泊，
牠們也生活在陸地上，
青蛙可以生活在陸地和水裡。

讓我們仔細瞧瞧青蛙吧！

青蛙有長長的後腳，可以幫助牠們跳得很高；
青蛙有蹼足，可以幫助牠們游得很快。
青蛙有濕潤、平滑的皮膚，
青蛙可以用牠們的長舌頭捕捉昆蟲。

但青蛙的外觀並非一直如此，
當青蛙還是幼兒時，牠們看起來相當不同。

這是什麼？
這是一隻蝌蚪，牠是一隻幼蛙。

青蛙在冬天產卵，
蝌蚪由卵中孵化出來，
蝌蚪只能在水裡生活，牠們像魚一樣，有長長的尾巴。

漸漸地，蝌蚪長出腿，
牠們的尾巴慢慢地消失。
數周後，牠們長為成蛙，
接著，青蛙就可以到陸地上生活。

Check Understanding 文意測驗

1 以下圖片是哪個身體部位？

　a **tongue** 舌頭　　　　**b** **webbed feet** 蹼足

2 青蛙能生長在哪裡？　**c**

　a 僅陸地　　　　**b** 僅水裡　　　　**c** 陸地和水裡

3 青蛙用長長的後腳來做什麼？　**c**

　a 游泳　　　　**b** 捕蟲　　　　**c** 跳高

4 ＿＿＿＿＿＿是幼蛙。　**a**

　a 蝌蚪　　　　**b** 蟲子　　　　**c** 尾巴

● 回答問題

1 When do frogs lay eggs? 青蛙何時產卵？
⇨Frogs lay eggs in **winter**. 青蛙在冬季產卵。

2 How do frogs use their long tongues? 青蛙如何使用牠們的長舌頭？
⇨ Frogs **catch** **bugs** with their long tongues. 青蛙用牠們的長舌頭抓蟲子。

Vocabulary and Grammar Builder 字彙與文法練習

A 看圖填空：依照圖片選出正確的單字。

1 Frogs live in **ponds**, lakes, and swamps. 青蛙生活在池塘、湖泊和沼澤。

2 Frogs can **leap** high. 青蛙能跳得很高。

3 Frogs **catch bugs** with their long tongues. 青蛙用牠們的長舌頭抓蟲子。

4 **Tadpoles** hatch from eggs. 蝌蚪由卵中孵出。

B Dry（乾）或Wet（濕）？圈出正確的單字，並填入空格中。

1 Frogs have ＿＿**wet**＿＿ skin. 青蛙有濕潤的皮膚。
　　dry　(wet)

2 Frogs have ＿＿**webbed**＿＿ feet. 青蛙有蹼足。
　　web　(webbed)

3 Frogs also have wet, ＿＿**smooth**＿＿ skin. 青蛙也有光滑的皮膚。
　　(smooth)　webbed

4 Baby frogs look ＿＿**different**＿＿ from adult frogs. 幼蛙看起來與成蛙不同。
　　(different)　alike

119

The Three Little Pigs

三隻小豬的故事

Reading Focus 閱讀焦點

- What animals appear in the story? 故事中出現了哪些動物？
- What did the three little pigs build their houses with? 這三隻小豬用什麼材料建造房子？
- What happened to the big bad wolf? 壞心大野狼的下場是什麼？

Key Words 關鍵字彙

Who Is in the Story?
故事裡出現哪些角色？

the first little pig
第一隻小豬

the second little pig
第二隻小豬

the third little pig
第三隻小豬

the big bad wolf
壞心大野狼

Houses
房屋

chimney
煙囪

roof
屋頂

straw house
稻草屋

stick house
木屋

brick house
磚瓦屋

straw
稻草

stick
樹枝

brick
磚頭

Power Verbs 核心動詞

decide to
決定去……

They **decided to** leave.
牠們決定離開。

build
建造

The little pig **built** a house.
這隻小豬建造了一間房屋。

knock
敲

He **knocked** on the door.
牠敲了敲門。

huff (= puff)
吹氣

The wolf **huffed** and **puffed**.
這隻野狼吹呀吹。

blow down
吹倒

The wind **blew down** the house.
風吹倒了房屋。

run away
逃跑

The wolf **ran away**.
這隻野狼逃跑了。

Word Families 相關字彙

climb up
爬上

He **climbed up** on the roof.
牠爬上屋頂。

jump down
跳下

He **jumped down** the chimney.
牠跳下煙囪。

fall into
掉進

He **fell into** the hot water.
牠掉進熱水裡。

scream
尖叫

He **screamed** loudly.
牠大聲尖叫。

yell
吼叫

He **yelled** loudly.
牠大聲吼叫。

The Three Little Pigs 三隻小豬的故事

很久很久以前，有三隻小豬。
有一天，牠們決定離家，去建造自己的家園。

第一隻小豬用稻草蓋了一間屋子；
第二隻小豬用樹枝蓋了一間屋子；
第三隻小豬用堅硬的磚頭蓋了一間屋子。

樹林裡住著一隻壞心的大野狼，
有一天，野狼看到第一隻小豬在牠的稻草屋裡，
野狼心想：「真是太美味啦！那隻豬仔一定很可口！」

很快地，壞心的大野狼來到稻草屋前，
牠敲了敲門，說道：「小豬仔啊，小豬仔！讓我進來坐坐吧！」
小豬回答：「不行！我對下巴上的鬍子發誓，絕對不讓你進來！」
野狼說：「那我就吹呀吹，把你的房子給吹垮！」
大野狼一陣陣地吹氣，果真把稻草屋給吹倒了。

第一隻小豬逃到第二隻小豬的房子，
把壞心大野狼的事都告訴了牠。

就在那時，壞心大野狼來到木屋前，
牠敲了敲門，說道：「小豬仔啊，小豬仔！讓我進來坐坐吧！」
小豬回答：「不行！我對下巴上的鬍子發誓，絕對不讓你進來！」
野狼說：「那我就吹呀吹，把你的房子給吹垮！」

大野狼一陣陣地吹氣，果真把木屋給吹倒了。

這兩隻小豬逃到第三隻小豬的房子，
把壞心大野狼的事都告訴了牠。

就在那時，壞心大野狼來到磚瓦屋前，
牠敲了敲門，說道：「小豬仔啊，小豬仔！讓我進來坐坐吧！」
小豬回答：「不行！我對下巴上的鬍子發誓，絕對不讓你進來！」
野狼說：「那我就吹呀吹，把你的房子給吹垮！」.
大野狼一陣陣地吹氣，吹呀吹的，卻始終無法把磚瓦屋吹倒。

小豬說道：「我的房子對你而言太堅固了，你是沒辦法吹垮的！」

壞心大野狼看著磚瓦屋，
發現屋頂上有一個煙囪，
牠想著：「啊哈！有辦法了！」牠對自己說：
「我要爬上屋頂，從煙囪進入房子裡！然後我就可以吃掉這三隻豬仔了！」
於是壞心大野狼跳下煙囪。

但是第三隻小豬非常聰明，
牠在壁爐裡面放了裝滿沸水的大鍋子。
噗通一聲！
壞心大野狼掉進了滾燙的熱水中，
牠尖叫大吼著逃走，
這三隻小豬從此過著快樂的日子。

Check Understanding　文意測驗

1　以下圖片是哪種房屋？

　　a house of straw (= straw house) 稻草屋　　　　**b** house of bricks (= brick house) 磚瓦屋

2　第三隻小豬用什麼建造房子？　**a**

　　a 磚頭　　　　　　　　**b** 稻草　　　　　　　　**c** 樹枝

3　壞心大野狼對第一隻跟第二隻小豬的房子做了什麼？　**b**

　　a 牠燒了它們　　　　　**b** 牠吹垮它們　　　　　**c** 牠推倒它們

4　誰的房子最堅固？　**c**

　　a 第一隻小豬的稻草屋

　　b 第二隻小豬的木屋

　　c 第三隻小豬的磚瓦屋

5　野狼想從_____進去第三隻小豬的房子。　**a**

　　a 煙囪　　　　　　　　**b** 門　　　　　　　　　**c** 窗戶

6　第三隻小豬在火爐裡放了什麼？　**b**

　　a 堅硬的磚頭　　　　　**b** 一鍋沸騰的水　　　　**c** 堅固的樹枝

● 回答問題

1　What did the three little pigs make their houses with?　這三隻小豬用什麼建造牠們的房子？

　　⇨ They made their houses with <u>straw</u>, <u>sticks</u>, and <u>bricks</u>.　牠們用稻草樹枝和磚頭建造牠們的房子。

2　Where did the big bad wolf fall into?　壞心大野狼掉進哪裡？

　　⇨ He <u>fell</u> <u>into</u> a pot of boiling <u>hot</u> <u>water</u>.　牠掉進一鍋沸騰的熱水裡。

Vocabulary and **Grammar** Builder　字彙與文法練習

A 看圖填空：依照圖片選出正確的單字。

1　The <u>first</u> pig built a house with straw.　第一隻小豬用稻草蓋了一間屋子。

2　The second little pig built a house with <u>sticks</u>.　第二隻小豬用樹枝蓋了一間屋子。

3　The third pig built a house with <u>bricks</u>.　第三隻小豬用堅硬的磚頭蓋了一間屋子。

4　The wolf fell into the <u>boiling</u> hot water.　這隻野狼掉進熱水裡。

B 現在式knock或是過去式knocked？圈出正確的單字，並填入空格中。

1　The big bad wolf ___**knocked**___ on the door.　壞心大野狼敲了敲門。
　　（knocked）knockt

2　The big bad wolf ___**blew**___ down the house.　壞心大野狼把房子吹垮了。
　　blowed （blew）

3　The big bad wolf yelled and ___**ran**___ away.　壞心大野狼大吼著逃走。
　　runned （ran）

4　The big bad wolf ___**jumped**___ down the chimney.　壞心大野狼跳下煙囪。
　　（jumped）jumpped

Reading Focus 閱讀焦點

- What are the numbers from 11 to 20? 11到20的數字有哪些？
- Can you count by twos? 你能兩個兩個一數嗎？
- How many things are in a pair? 哪些物品是成對出現？

Key Words 關鍵字彙

Numbers
數字

1	2	3	4	5
one	two	three	four	five
6	7	8	9	10
six	seven	eight	nine	ten
11	12	13	14	15
eleven	twelve	thirteen	fourteen	fifteen
16	17	18	19	20
sixteen	seventeen	eighteen	nineteen	twenty

Skip-Counting
跳數

| 1 | ② two 二 | 3 | ④ four 四 | 5 | ⑥ six 六 | 7 | ⑧ eight 八 | 9 | ⑩ ten 十 |
| 11 | ⑫ twelve 十二 | 13 | ⑭ fourteen 十四 | 15 | ⑯ sixteen 十六 | 17 | ⑱ eighteen 十八 | 19 | ⑳ twenty 二十 |

Power Verbs 核心動詞

skip-count
跳數

find out
找出

Let's **skip-count** by twos.
讓我們兩個兩個跳數。

Let's **find out** the answer.
讓我們找出答案。

be grouped
被分組

come in
出現

wear
穿著

They **are grouped** by twos.
它們被兩個兩個分成一組。

Shoes **come in** pairs.
鞋子都是成對出現。

She is **wearing** a pink dress.
她正穿著粉紅色洋裝。

Word Families 相關字彙：成對的東西

Body Pairs
成對的身體部分

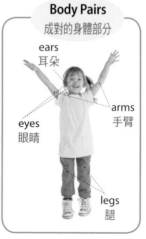

ears 耳朵

arms 手臂

eyes 眼睛

legs 腿

Clothing Pairs
成對的穿戴物品

socks 襪子

shoes 鞋子

pants 褲子

gloves 手套

glasses 眼鏡

Skip-Counting 跳數

讓我們數到十，
一、二、三、四、五、六、七、八、九、十。
我們一個接一個地把這些數字數出來。

讓我們兩個兩個一數，來數這些數字吧，
二、四、六、八、十。
兩個兩個一數，比一個一個數快很多。

當我們兩個兩個一數，我們正在「跳數」，
讓我們兩個兩個一數跳數到二十，
二、四、六、八、十、
十二、十四、十六、十八、二十。

看看這些鞋子，
讓我們找出這裡有幾雙鞋。

這些鞋子以兩個為一組，我們稱之為「一對」。

你能兩個兩個一數來數清它們嗎？
2、4、6、8、10、12。
那裡有幾雙鞋子？
有十二雙鞋子。
那裡有幾對鞋子？
有六對鞋子。

許多東西會以兩個，或成雙成對的方式出現。
你有一對眼睛；
你有一雙手臂；
你有一雙腿。

人們穿一雙襪子；
人們戴一對手套；
有些人戴一副眼鏡。

Check Understanding 文意測驗

1 以下圖片是何種成對的物品？
  a a pair of <u>glasses</u> 一副眼鏡   b a pair of <u>socks</u> 一雙襪子

2 一對物品的數量有幾個？ **b**
  a 一   b 二   c 三

3 哪些數字是兩個兩個一數？ **b**
  a 1, 2, 3, 4, 5   b 2, 4, 6, 8, 10   c 5, 10, 15, 20, 25

4 我們有一對_____。 **a**
  a 耳朵   b 手指   c 嘴巴

● 回答問題

1 What are the numbers from 11 to 15? 11到15之間的數字有哪些？
  ⇨ They are <u>eleven</u>, <u>twelve</u>, <u>thirteen</u>, <u>fourteen</u>, and <u>fifteen</u>. 11, 12, 13, 14, 15。

2 What are the numbers from 16 to 20? 16到20之間的數字有哪些？
  ⇨ They are <u>sixteen</u>, <u>seventeen</u>, <u>eighteen</u>, <u>nineteen</u>, and <u>twenty</u>. 16, 17, 18, 19, 20。

Vocabulary and Grammar Builder 字彙與文法練習

A 看圖填空：依照圖片選出正確的單字。

1 Let's <u>skip-count</u> by twos. 讓我們兩個兩個跳數。

2 He has a <u>pair</u> of gloves. 他有一對手套。

3 They are <u>grouped</u> by twos. 它們被兩兩分組。

4 Shoes <u>come in</u> pairs. 鞋子都是成雙出現。

B 一個或更多？圈出正確的單字，並填入空格中。

1 You have a pair of ___**eyes**___ . 你有一對眼睛。
   eye (eyes)

2 You have a pair of ___**arms**___ . 你有一雙手臂。
   arm (arms)

3 People wear a pair of ___**socks**___ . 人們穿一雙襪子。
   sock (socks)

4 Some people wear a pair of ___**glasses**___ . 有些人戴一副眼鏡。
   glass (glasses)

125

Unit 11 Colors
色彩的奧妙

Reading Focus 閱讀焦點

- How many colors can you name? 你能列舉出幾種顏色？
- What are warm colors? 哪些顏色是屬於暖色系？
- What are cool colors? 哪些顏色是屬於冷色系？

Key Words 關鍵字彙

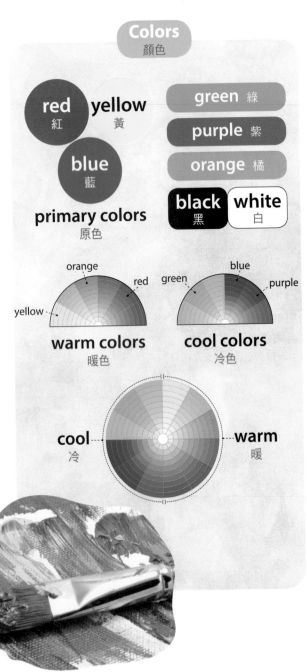

Colors 顏色

red 紅 yellow 黃 blue 藍
green 綠 purple 紫 orange 橘
black 黑 white 白

primary colors 原色

orange red yellow
warm colors 暖色

green blue purple
cool colors 冷色

cool 冷 ——— warm 暖

Power Verbs 核心動詞

look around
環顧四周

Look around you.
環顧你的四周。

name
列舉

Name your favorite color.
列舉出你喜歡的顏色。

mix
混合

Let's mix the colors.
讓我們將顏色混合。

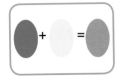

combine
結合

Combine red and yellow.
把紅色和黃色相結合。

Word Families : Sensations 相關字彙：感覺

exciting
令人興奮的

The game is very exciting.
這比賽相當令人興奮。

excited
興奮的

I feel excited when
I play the game.
當我參加比賽時，我感到興奮。

relaxing
令人放鬆的

Staying at home
is relaxing.
待在家是令人
放鬆的。

relaxed
放鬆的

I feel relaxed when
I listen to music.
當我聽音樂時 我
感到放鬆。

calm
平靜

The sea was
very calm.
這片海非常
平靜。

Colors 色彩的奧妙

環顧你的四周，
你有看見藍天嗎？有看見一些綠草地嗎？
有看見一串香蕉嗎？
色彩隨處可見，
你能列舉出幾種顏色呢？

色彩中有三種原色，
它們是紅色、黃色和藍色。

我們可以混合這些原色，
然後就能變化成其他顏色。

混合藍色和黃色，就會變成綠色；
混合藍色和紅色，就會變成紫色；

混合紅色和黃色，就會變成橘色。

混合紅色、藍色和黃色，就會變成黑色。
有些顏色是「暖色系」，
紅色、黃色和橘色是暖色。
它們使我們感到興奮和快樂。

有些顏色是「冷色系」，
藍色、綠色和紫色是冷色。
它們使我們感到放鬆。

你喜歡暖色、令人感到興奮的顏色，
還是冷色、令人感到平靜的顏色呢？

Check Understanding 文意測驗

1　以下圖片呈現何種顏色？
　　a **orange (warm color)** 橘（暖色）　　　　b **green (cool color)** 綠（冷色）

2　哪個顏色是原色？ **b**
　　a 綠　　　　　　　b 紅　　　　　　　c 黑

3　冷色會讓人有怎樣的感覺？ **b**
　　a 興奮　　　　　　b 放鬆　　　　　　c 憤怒

4　_____色使人們感到興奮。 **c**
　　a 熱　　　　　　　b 冷　　　　　　　c 暖

● 回答問題

1　What are the three primary colors? 三原色是指哪三種顏色？
　　⇨ They are <u>red</u>, <u>yellow</u>, and <u>blue</u>. 紅色、黃色和藍色。

2　What are some warm colors? 暖色系的顏色有哪些？
　　⇨ They are <u>red</u>, <u>yellow</u>, and <u>orange</u>. 紅色、黃色和橘色。

Vocabulary and Grammar Builder 字彙與文法練習

Ⓐ 看圖填空：依照圖片選出正確的單字。

1　Yellow is a <u>**primary**</u> color. 黃色是原色。

2　<u>**Mix**</u> blue and red to make purple. 把藍色和紅色混合成紫色。

3　Can you <u>**name**</u> some warm colors? 你能列舉一些暖色系的顏色嗎？

4　Blue is a cool, <u>**calm**</u> color. 藍色是冷調、平靜的顏色。

Ⓑ Excited（興奮的）或Exciting（令人興奮的）？圈出正確的單字，並填入空格中。

1　The game is very _____**exciting**_____. 這場比賽非常激動人心。
　　excited　(exciting)

2　Warm colors make us feel _____**excited**_____. 暖色系顏色使我們感覺興奮。
　　(excited)　exciting

3　Staying at home is _____**relaxing**_____. 待在家是令人放鬆的。
　　(relaxing)　feel relaxed

4　Cool colors make us feel _____**relaxed**_____. 冷色系顏色使我們感到放鬆。
　　(relaxed)　relaxing

127

Musical Instruments and Their Families

樂器和樂器家族

Reading Focus 閱讀焦點

- What are some musical instruments? 樂器有哪些？
- How do you play these instruments? 你要如何演奏這些樂器？

Key Words 關鍵字彙

Keyboard Family 鍵盤樂器家族

key 鍵

piano 鋼琴   **organ** 風琴

Woodwind Family 木管樂器家族

flute 長笛

clarinet 豎笛

String Family 弦樂器家族

bow 弓

violin 小提琴   **viola** 中提琴   **cello** 大提琴

Brass Family 銅管樂器家族

trumpet 喇叭

trombone 長號

Percussion Family 打擊樂器家族

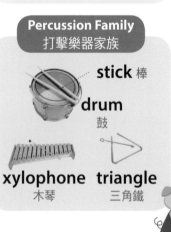

stick 棒

drum 鼓

xylophone 木琴   **triangle** 三角鐵

Power Verbs 核心動詞

look alike 看起來很像

Some instruments look alike.
有些樂器外觀很相似。

strike 敲

Strike the piano keys.
敲鋼琴的琴鍵。

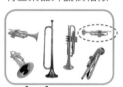

belong to 屬於……

The trumpet belongs to the brass family.
喇叭屬於銅管樂器家族。

blow 吹

Blow air into the flute.
將氣吹進長笛裡。

Word Families : Tools for Musical Instruments

相關字彙：樂器演奏工具

keyboard 鍵盤 ⟹ A piano has a keyboard.
鋼琴有鍵盤。

string 弦 ⟹ A violin has strings.
小提琴有弦。

bow 弓 ⟹ You play the violin with a bow.
你用弓來演奏小提琴。

stick 棒 ⟹ You hit the drum with a stick.
你用棒子來打鼓。

Musical Instruments and Their Families 樂器和樂器家族

樂器有許多種類，
有些樂器外觀很相似，
這些樂器屬於相同的家族。
讓我們來看看這些樂器家族吧！

你知道鍵盤樂器有哪些嗎？
鋼琴！沒錯！
鋼琴有鍵盤，風琴也有鍵盤，
它們都屬於鍵盤樂器家族，
你要敲打琴鍵來彈奏它們。

你知道哪些樂器有弦嗎？
小提琴？大提琴？還是中提琴？
它們都屬於弦樂器家族，
你要用弓來演奏它們。

長笛和豎笛屬於木管樂器家族，
喇叭和長號屬於銅管樂器家族，
你靠吹氣進去來演奏它們。

鼓、木琴和三角鐵屬於打擊樂器家族，
你要使用棒子去演奏它們。

Chapter
3

Unit
12

Musical Instruments and Their Families

Check Understanding 文意測驗

1 以下圖片是哪種樂器？
   a **flute** 長笛　　　　　　**b** **trumpet** 喇叭

2 你要如何演奏長號？ **b**
   a 敲打琴鍵　　　　　**b** 吹氣進去　　　　　**c** 用棒子敲打

3 中提琴屬於何種樂器？ **b**
   a 木管樂器　　　　　**b** 弦樂器　　　　　　**c** 銅管樂器

4 _____是一種打擊樂器。 **a**
   a 木琴　　　　　　　**b** 中提琴　　　　　　**c** 鋼琴

● 回答問題

1 What musical instruments have strings? 哪些樂器有弦？
   ⇨ The <u>violin</u>, <u>viola</u>, and <u>cello</u> have strings. 小提琴、中提琴和大提琴有弦。

2 How do you play the cello? 你要如何演奏大提琴？
   ⇨ You play the cello with a <u>bow</u>. 你用弓來演奏大提琴。

Vocabulary and Grammar Builder 字彙與文法練習

A 看圖填空：依照圖片選出正確的單字。

1 <u>Strike</u> the piano keys. 敲打鋼琴琴鍵。

2 <u>Blow</u> air into the clarinet. 把氣吹進豎笛裡。

3 The piano and organ <u>look alike</u>. 鋼琴和風琴看起來很像。

4 The trumpet <u>belongs to</u> the brass family. 喇叭屬於銅管樂器家族。

B Strings（弦）或Sticks（棒）？圈出正確的單字，並填入空格中。

1 The piano has a ____**keyboard**____. 鋼琴有鍵盤。
   (keyboard)　string

2 The violin has ____**strings**____. 小提琴有弦。
   (strings)　sticks

3 Play the violin with a ____**bow**____. 用弓來演奏小提琴。
   stick　(bow)

4 Hit the drum with a ____**stick**____. 用棒子來打鼓。
   (stick)　bow

A 看圖填空：依照圖片選出正確的單字。

1 The entire country celebrates <u>national holidays</u>. 全國上下都會慶祝國定假日。

2 The Native Americans helped the <u>Pilgrims</u>. 美洲原住民幫助這些清教徒前輩移民。

3 A map is a drawing of a <u>real</u> place. 地圖是實地的圖示。

4 Antarctica is at the <u>bottom</u> of Earth. 南極洲在地球的底端。

B 圈出正確的單字，並填入空格中。

1 Tim is ____<u>having</u>____ a party today. 提姆今天將舉辦一個生日派對。
       have (having)

2 Squanto ____<u>showed</u>____ the Pilgrims how to hunt. 斯夸托教他們如何打獵。
       (showed) stayed

3 The fire station is ____<u>east</u>____ of the house. 消防局在房子的東方。
       (east) west

4 The school is ____<u>south</u>____ of the house. 學校在房子的南方。
       north (south)

C 選出正確的單字填空，以完成句子。

1 We <u>celebrate</u> special days every year. 我們每年都會慶祝特別的日子。

2 The <u>entire</u> country celebrates a national holidays. 全國上下都會慶祝國定假日。

3 People give <u>each other</u> gifts on Christmas. 人們在聖誕節會互送禮物。

4 Americans <u>honor</u> Independence Day. 美國人會紀念獨立紀念日。

5 The first <u>Thanksgiving</u> was celebrated by the Pilgrims.
   最早的感恩節慶祝活動，始於清教徒前輩移民。

6 Squanto <u>stayed</u> with the Pilgrims to help them.
   斯夸托留在清教徒前輩移民身邊幫助他們。

7 The Pilgrims <u>invited</u> the Native Americans to their meal.
   清教徒前輩移民邀請美洲原住民們共享佳餚。

8 For three days, they had a big <u>festival</u>. 他們連續三天舉行了盛大的慶典。

D 選出正確的單字填空，以完成句子。

1 A map can <u>show</u> many places. 地圖可以顯示很多地方。

2 There are four main <u>directions</u>. 有四個主要的方位。

3 They are north, south, <u>east</u>, and west. 分別是北方、南方、東方和西方。

4 If you follow the <u>arrow</u>, you can go that direction.
   如果跟著箭頭方向走，就能朝著那個方向前進。

5 There are seven <u>continents</u> on Earth. 地球上有七塊大陸。

6 There are five <u>oceans</u> on Earth. 地球上有五個大洋。

7 <u>Asia</u> is the largest continent. 亞洲是最大的大陸。

8 North America and South America are <u>connected</u> to each other.
   北美洲和南美洲互相連接。

A 看圖填空：依照圖片選出正確的單字。

1 Plants' roots <u>hold</u> water. 植物的根可以儲存水分。

2 Some plants <u>catch</u> insects. 有些植物會捕捉昆蟲。

3 Fish use their <u>fins</u> to swim. 魚類使用牠們的鰭來游泳。

4 Tadpoles <u>hatch</u> from eggs. 蝌蚪從卵孵化。

B 圈出正確的單字，並填入空格中。

1 Tundra is a ____**snowy**____ place. 凍原是有雪的地方。
        sunny   (snowy)

2 The rafflesia can be more than one meter ____**wide**____. 大王花可寬達一公尺。
        tall   (wide)

3 Sharks have large ____**jaws**____. 鯊魚有很大的下顎。
        nostrils   (jaws)

4 Frogs and tadpoles look ____**different**____. 青蛙和蝌蚪看起來很不一樣。
        alike   (different)

C 選出正確的單字填空，以完成句子。

1 There are many tall trees in a <u>rainforest</u>. 雨林裡有許多高大的樹木。

2 <u>Ferns</u> and flowers grow on the forest floor. 蕨類植物和花朵生長於森林地表。

3 Many desert plant have thick <u>stems</u>. 許多沙漠植物有很肥厚的莖。

4 <u>Tundra</u> is a cold, snowy place. 凍原是寒冷有雪的地方。

5 The <u>redwood</u> tree is the tallest tree in the world. 紅杉樹是世界上最高大的樹。

6 The <u>rafflesia</u> is the biggest flower in the world. 大王花是世界上最大的花。

7 The sundew plant's leaves are covered with <u>sticky</u> hairs. 毛氈苔的葉子被分泌黏液的毛覆蓋。

8 The Venus flytrap and sundew plant are <u>insect-eating</u> plants.
捕蠅草和毛氈苔是食蟲植物。

D 選出正確的單字填空，以完成句子。

1 Fish, crabs, sharks, and dolphins are all <u>ocean animals</u>.
魚類、螃蟹、鯊魚和海豚是海洋動物。

2 Fish use their fins and <u>tails</u> to swim. 魚類用牠們的鰭和尾來游泳。

3 Sharks use their <u>nostrils</u> to smell. 鯊魚用鼻孔嗅聞。

4 The great white shark is the most <u>dangerous</u> shark. 大白鯊是最危險的鯊魚種類。

5 Frogs can live both <u>on land</u> and in the water. 青蛙可以生活在陸地和水裡。

6 Frogs can <u>catch bugs</u> with their long tongues. 青蛙可以用牠們的長舌頭捕捉昆蟲。

7 Frogs have <u>webbed</u> feet to help them swim well. 青蛙有蹼足來幫助他們游泳。

8 Frogs <u>lay eggs</u> in winter. 青蛙在冬天產卵。

Ⓐ 看圖填空：依照圖片選出正確的單字。

1 The third pig **built** a house with bricks. 第三隻小豬用磚頭蓋了一棟房屋。。

2 Let's **skip-count** by twos. 讓我們兩個兩個跳數。

3 **Mix** blue and red to make purple. 把藍色和紅色混合成紫色。

4 **Blow** air into the flute. 將氣吹進長笛裡。

Ⓑ 圈出正確的單字，並填入空格中。

1 The big bad wolf ___**blew**___ down the house. 壞心大野狼把房子吹垮了。
   blowed (blew)

2 Some people wear a pair of ___**glasses**___. 有些人戴一副眼鏡。
   glass (glasses)

3 Cool colors make us feel ___**relaxed**___. 冷色系顏色使我們感覺放鬆。
   (relaxed) relaxing

4 Play the cello with a ___**bow**___. 用弓來演奏大提琴。
   stick (bow)

Ⓒ 選出正確的單字填空，以完成句子。

1 The first little pig built a house with **straw**. 第一隻小豬用稻草蓋了一間房屋。

2 The second little pig built a house with **sticks**. 第二隻小豬用樹枝蓋了一間房屋。

3 The third little pig built a house with hard **bricks**. 第三隻小豬用堅硬的磚頭蓋了一間房屋。

4 The big bad wolf **fell into** the boiling hot water.
   壞心大野狼掉進滾燙的熱水中。

5 Counting by twos is much **faster** than counting by ones.
   兩個兩個一數，比一個一個數快很多。

6 When we count by twos, we are "**skip-counting**."
   當我們兩個兩個一數，我們正在「跳數」。

7 Many things come in groups of twos, or **pairs**. 許多東西會以兩個，或成雙成對的方式出現。

8 Shoes **come in** pairs. 鞋子都是成雙出現。

Ⓓ 選出正確的單字填空，以完成句子。

1 There are three **primary** colors. 原色有三種。

2 We can **mix** the primary colors together. 我們可以混合這些原色。

3 Red, yellow, and orange are **warm** colors. 紅色、黃色和橘色是暖色。

4 Blue, green, and purple are **cool** colors. 藍色、綠色和紫色是冷色。

5 The piano and organ are in the **keyboard** family. 鋼琴和風琴屬於鍵盤樂器家族。

6 The violin and cello belong to the **string** family. 小提琴和大提琴屬於弦樂器家族。

7 The flute and clarinet belong to the **woodwind** family. 長笛和豎笛屬於木管樂器家族。

8 The trumpet and trombone belong to the **brass** family. 喇叭和長號屬於銅管樂器家族。

Authors

Michael A. Putlack

Michael A. Putlack graduated from Tufts University in Medford, Massachusetts, USA, where he got his B.A. in History and English and his M.A. in History. He has written a number of books for children, teenagers, and adults.

e-Creative Contents

A creative group that develops English contents and products for ESL and EFL students.

FUN學 美國各學科初級課本

新生入門英語閱讀 ②

作 者	Michael A. Putlack & e-Creative Contents
譯 者	丁宥暄
編 輯	賴祖兒／丁宥暄
主 編	丁宥暄
內文排版	謝青秀／林書玉
封面設計	林書玉
製程管理	洪巧玲
出 版 者	寂天文化事業股份有限公司
電 話	+886-(0)2-2365-9739
傳 真	+886-(0)2-2365-9835
網 址	www.icosmos.com.tw
讀者服務	onlineservice@icosmos.com.tw
出版日期	2020 年 9 月 二版再刷 (080203)

國家圖書館出版品預行編目資料

Fun學美國各學科初級課本：新生入門英語閱讀 /
Michael A. Putlack, e-Creative Contents著.
-- 二版. -- [臺北市] : 寂天文化, 2018.07-
　冊；　公分
ISBN 978-986-318-715-8(第1冊：平裝附光碟片)
ISBN 978-986-318-716-5(第2冊：平裝附光碟片)

1.英語 2.讀本

805.18　　　　　　　　　　　　107010450

FÜN學
美國各學科初級課本
新生入門英語閱讀 二版

AMERiCAN
SCHOOL
TEXTBOOK

Reading
Key BASIC

WORKBOOK
練習本

A Write the meaning of each word and phrase in Chinese.

1 special _____   21 Father's Day _____
2 special day _____   22 father _____
3 have a party _____ 23 national holiday _____
4 be coming _____   24 entire _____
5 will _____   25 Christmas _____
6 give _____   26 important _____
7 present _____   27 holiday _____
8 everyone _____   28 each other _____
9 have _____   29 gift _____
10 cake _____   30 Thanksgiving _____
11 ice cream _____   31 another _____
12 birthday _____   32 American _____
13 celebrate _____   33 share _____
14 every year _____   34 special food _____
15 family _____   35 friend _____
16 with a cake _____ 36 also _____
17 Children's Day _____ 37 honor _____
18 children _____   38 Independence Day _____
19 Mother's Day _____ 39 parade _____
20 mother _____   40 firework(s) _____

B Choose the word that best completes each sentence.

birthdays	celebrate	Thanksgiving	Christmas

1 We _____ special days every year.

2 Many families celebrate _____ with a cake.

3 People give each other gifts on _____.

4 Americans share special foods on _____.

▶ B, C大題解答請參照主冊課文
A大題解答請參照Word List（主冊P. 93）

Tim is having a _____ today.

His friends are _____ to his house.

They will give him _____.

Everyone will have _____ and ice cream.

What is this _____ day?

It's Tim's _____.

There are many special _____.

We celebrate special days _____ _____.

Many families _____ birthdays with a cake.

Children's Day is a special day for _____.

Mother's Day is a special day for _____.

Father's Day is a special day for _____.

There are also many _____ holidays.

The entire _____ celebrates these days.

_____ is one important holiday.

People give each other _____ on that day.

Thanksgiving is another big _____.

Americans _____ special food with their family and friends.

Americans also _____ Independence Day.

They celebrate the country's birthday with _____ and fireworks.

4

The First Thanksgiving

A Write the meaning of each word and phrase in Chinese.

1 the first _____
2 Thanksgiving _____
3 America _____
4 gather together _____
5 meal _____
6 be celebrated by _____
7 the Pilgrims _____
8 group _____
9 for _____
10 religion _____
11 sail _____
12 ship _____
13 called _____
14 the *Mayflower* _____
15 later _____
16 finally _____
17 land in _____
18 snowy _____
19 almost _____

20 half of _____
21 die _____
22 during _____
23 meet _____
24 some _____
25 Native American _____
26 Squanto _____
27 stay with _____
28 show _____
29 how to _____
30 how to fish _____
31 how to hunt _____
32 how to grow food _____
33 lots of _____
34 food _____
35 thank _____
36 big meal _____
37 invite _____
38 festival _____

B Choose the word that best completes each sentence.

Pilgrims	showed	celebrated	religion

1 The first Thanksgiving was _____ by the Pilgrims.

2 The _____ were a group of people from England.

3 Pilgrims went to America for their _____.

4 Squanto _____ the Pilgrims how to grow food.

5

Thanksgiving is a big holiday in _____.

Families _____ together and have a special meal.

The first Thanksgiving was _____ by the Pilgrims.

The Pilgrims were a group of people from _____.

They went to America for their _____.

They _____ on a ship called the *Mayflower*.

Two months later, they _____ landed in America.

It was the winter of _____.

The winter was very _____ and snowy.

Almost _____ of the Pilgrims died during the winter.

In spring, they met some _____ Americans.

They helped the _____.

One Native American, Squanto, could _____ English.

Squanto _____ with the Pilgrims to help them.

He _____ them how to fish.

He showed them how to _____.

He showed them how to _____ food.

That fall, the Pilgrims had _____ _____ food.

The Pilgrims _____ God.

They thanked the Native _____, too.

They made a big _____.

They _____ the Native Americans to their meal.

For three days, they had a big _____.

That was the _____ Thanksgiving.

What Is a Map?

A Write the meaning of each word and phrase in Chinese.

1	map	23	find
2	look at	24	main
3	house	25	four (main) directions
4	building	26	north
5	drawing	27	south
6	real	28	east
7	place	29	west
8	real place	30	picture
9	show	31	like
10	entire	32	letter
11	the entire world	33	if
12	country	34	follow
13	city	35	arrow
14	just	36	now
15	neighborhood	37	again
16	thing	38	south of
17	point to	39	police station
18	school	40	north of
19	near	41	fire station
20	sometimes	42	east of
21	use	43	church
22	direction	44	west of

B Choose the word that best completes each sentence.

main	drawing	directions	north

1 A map is a _____ of a real place.

2 Sometimes, we use _____ to find a place.

3 There are four _____ directions.

4 They are _____, south, east, and west.

Look _____ the map.

You can see many _____, trees, and buildings.

A map is a _____ of a real place.

A map can show many _____.

It can show the _____ world.

It can show a _____ or a city.

Or it can just show a small _____.

A _____ helps you know where things are.

_____ to the school on the map.

Where is it? The school is _____ the house.

Sometimes, we use _____ to find a place.

There are four _____ directions.

They are north, _____, east, and west.

Many maps use a _____ like this.

The _____ N, S, E, and W show the directions:

north, south, east, and west.

If you follow the _____, you can go that direction.

Now, look at the map _____.

Where is the _____?

The school is _____ _____ the house.

The police station is _____ _____ the house.

The fire station is _____ _____ the house.

The church is _____ _____ the house.

8

A **Write the meaning of each word and phrase in Chinese.**

1 ocean _____

2 continent _____

3 map of the world _____

4 be made up of _____

5 body of land _____

6 body of water _____

7 live on _____

8 Asia _____

9 largest _____

10 Russia _____

11 China _____

12 Korea _____

13 Japan _____

14 Europe _____

15 be next to _____

16 England _____

17 France _____

18 Germany _____

19 Africa _____

20 be near _____

21 Egypt _____

22 South Africa _____

23 be located in _____

24 North America _____

25 South America _____

26 be connected to _____

27 each other _____

28 the United States _____

29 Canada _____

30 Brazil _____

31 Argentina _____

32 Australia _____

33 island _____

34 Antarctica _____

35 at the bottom of _____

36 be surrounded by _____

37 Pacific Ocean _____

38 biggest _____

39 on one side of _____

40 on the other side of _____

41 Atlantic Ocean _____

42 Indian Ocean _____

43 Antarctic Ocean _____

44 Arctic Ocean _____

B **Choose the word that best completes each sentence.**

island	made up of	continent	ocean

1 Earth is _____ continents and oceans.

2 A _____ is a very large body of land.

3 An _____ is a very large body of water.

4 Australia is an _____ continent.

Look at the map of the _____.

_____ is made up of continents and oceans.

A _____ is a very large body of land.

There are seven _____ on Earth.

An _____ is a very large body of water.

There are five _____ on Earth.

We _____ _____ a continent.

Asia is the _____ continent.

Russia, China, Korea, and Japan are in _____.

Europe is _____ _____ Asia.

England, France, and Germany are in _____.

Africa is _____ Europe and Asia.

Egypt and South Africa are located in _____.

North America and South America are _____ to each other.

The United States and Canada are _____ in North America.

Brazil and Argentina are located in _____ _____.

Australia is an _____ continent.

And Antarctica is at the _____ of Earth.

The continents are _____ by the oceans.

The _____ Ocean is the biggest ocean.

Asia is on _____ _____ of it.

North and South America are on _____ _____ _____ of it.

Where Do Plants Live?

A Write the meaning of each word and phrase in Chinese.

1 plant _____

2 live in _____

3 many places _____

4 rainforest _____

5 wet _____

6 get rain _____

7 tall _____

8 below _____

9 ferns _____

10 flowers _____

11 grow _____

12 forest floor _____

13 desert _____

14 dry _____

15 very little _____

16 such _____

17 desert plant _____

18 thick _____

19 stem _____

20 store _____

21 cactus _____

22 hold _____

23 if _____

24 rain _____

25 for a long time _____

26 even _____

27 tundra _____

28 snowy _____

29 close together _____

30 survive _____

B Choose the word that best completes each sentence.

desert	rainforest	tundra	cactus

1 There are many tall trees in a _____.

2 A _____ gets very little rain.

3 A _____ can hold water in its thick stem.

4 _____ is a cold, snowy place.

Plants live in many _____.

Many plants live in _____.

A rainforest is a hot, _____ place.

It _____ lots of rain.

There are many _____ trees in a rainforest.

They often have large _____.

Below the tall trees, there are _____ plants.

Ferns and flowers grow on the forest _____.

Some plants live in _____.

A desert is a hot, _____ place.

It gets very _____ rain.

How do plants grow in _____ a hot and dry place?

Many desert _____ have thick stems.

These help the plants _____ water.

A _____ is a desert plant.

It can hold water in its _____ stem.

So it can use the water later if it does not _____ for a long time.

Some plants even live in the _____.

Tundra is a _____, snowy place.

Plants there _____ _____ grow very tall.

And they grow _____ together.

This helps them _____ in the cold tundra.

A Write the meaning of each word and phrase in Chinese.

1 amazing _____

2 more than _____

3 type _____

4 redwood (tree) _____

5 tallest _____

6 in the world _____

7 grow in _____

8 California _____

9 USA _____

10 100 meters _____

11 rafflesia _____

12 jungle _____

13 one meter _____

14 wide _____

15 catch _____

16 insect _____

17 insect-eating plant _____

18 Venus flytrap _____

19 hold _____

20 juice _____

21 land on _____

22 quickly _____

23 close _____

24 trap _____

25 digest _____

26 sundew plant _____

27 be covered with _____

28 sticky _____

29 hair _____

30 slowly _____

31 pitcher plant _____

32 look like _____

33 pitcher _____

34 splash _____

35 fall into _____

36 cup-shaped _____

B Choose the word that best completes each sentence.

redwood	pitcher	rafflesia	trap

1 The _____ tree is the tallest tree in the world.

2 The _____ is the biggest flower in the world.

3 _____ plants have cup-shaped leaves.

4 The leaves of a Venus flytrap _____ insects.

There are more than 300,000 _____ of plants.

Some plants are _____.

The _____ tree is the tallest tree in the world.

It _____ in California in the USA.

Some redwoods can grow more than 100 _____ tall.

The rafflesia is the _____ flower in the world.

It grows in the _____ of Asia.

This flower can be more than one meter _____.

Some plants _____ insects.

They are _____ plants.

The Venus flytrap has special _____.

The leaves hold a sweet _____.

An insect lands on the _____.

Then, the leaf _____ closes.

The leaf _____ the insect.

Then, juices from the plant _____ it.

The _____ plant has special leaves, too.

The leaves are covered with _____ hairs.

An insect _____ on the sticky hairs.

Then, the leaf _____ closes.

Then, _____ from the plant digest it.

Pitcher plants have leaves that look like _____.

Splash! Insects fall into the _____ leaves.

Then, juices from the _____ digest them.

What Lives in an Ocean?

A Write the meaning of each word and phrase in Chinese.

1 ocean _____

2 sea _____

3 fish _____

4 crab _____

5 sea turtle _____

6 shark _____

7 dolphin _____

8 ocean animal _____

9 gills _____

10 breathe _____

11 fin _____

12 tail _____

13 swim _____

14 special _____

15 take a look _____

16 take a close look at _____

17 fast _____

18 jaw _____

19 sharp _____

20 teeth _____

21 hunt _____

22 well _____

23 blue water _____

24 sound _____

25 far away _____

26 from far away _____

27 nostril _____

28 smell _____

29 five hundred _____

30 kind _____

31 dangerous _____

32 great white shark _____

33 the most dangerous _____

34 attack _____

35 anything _____

36 even _____

B Choose the word that best completes each sentence.

gills	fins	sharp	attack

1 All fish live in water and have _____.

2 Fish use their _____ and tails to swim.

3 Sharks have large jaws with very _____ teeth.

4 The great white shark can _____ people.

An ocean is a very large _____.

Many plants and _____ live in the ocean.

Fish, crabs, sea turtles, sharks, and _____ are all ocean animals.

All fish live in _____ and have gills.

Gills help fish _____ in water.

Fish have _____ and tails, too.

They use their fins and _____ to swim.

Look at the _____!

Are they _____?

Yes, sharks are fish, but they are _____.

Let's take a _____ look at a shark.

Sharks have _____ and long fins.

These fins and tails help sharks _____ fast.

Sharks have large _____ with very sharp teeth.

The sharp _____ help sharks hunt fish well.

Sharks can see _____ in the blue water.

Sharks can hear sounds from _____ _____.

Sharks use their _____ to smell.

There are more than five _____ kinds of sharks.

Some sharks are very _____.

The great _____ shark is the most dangerous shark.

It _____ anything—even people!

How Frogs Grow and Change

A Write the meaning of each word and phrase in Chinese.

1 frog _____
2 grow _____
3 change _____
4 ribbit _____
5 pond _____
6 swamp _____
7 lake _____
8 land _____
9 both _____
10 on land _____
11 in the water _____
12 front leg _____
13 back leg _____
14 leap _____
15 webbed _____
16 webbed feet _____
17 wet _____
18 smooth _____
19 skin _____

20 catch _____
21 bug _____
22 tongue _____
23 always _____
24 look like _____
25 baby _____
26 look different _____
27 tadpole _____
28 baby frog _____
29 lay eggs _____
30 hatch _____
31 only _____
32 tail _____
33 gradually _____
34 develop _____
35 disappear _____
36 a few weeks _____
37 become _____
38 adult frog _____

B Choose the word that best completes each sentence.

leap	bugs	both	tadpoles

1 Frogs can live _____ on land and in the water.

2 Frogs can catch _____ with their long tongues.

3 Frogs have long back legs so they can _____ high.

4 _____ hatch from the eggs.

C **Listen to the passage and fill in the blanks.** 32

Ribbit, ribbit, _____.

Can you hear the _____?

Frogs live in many _____.

They live in ponds, _____, and lakes.

They also live on _____.

Frogs can live _____ on land and in the water.

Let's _____ a closer look at a frog.

Frogs have long _____ legs. These help frogs _____ well.

Frogs have _____ feet. These help frogs _____ well.

Frogs have wet, _____ skin.

And frogs can catch bugs with their long _____.

But they do not always look _____ that.

As _____, frogs look very different.

What is this?

It is a _____. It's a _____ frog.

Frogs _____ _____ in winter.

Tadpoles _____ from the eggs.

_____ only live in the water. They have long _____ like fish.

Gradually, tadpoles develop _____.

Their tails slowly _____.

After a few _____, they become adult frogs.

Then, they can live on _____.

18

The Three Little Pigs

A Write the meaning of each word and phrase in Chinese.

1 little pig _____
2 once upon a time _____
3 one day _____
4 decide to _____
5 own _____
6 the first _____
7 build _____
8 straw _____
9 with straw _____
10 the second _____
11 stick _____
12 the third _____
13 hard _____
14 brick _____
15 woods _____
16 bad _____
17 wolf _____
18 house of straw _____
19 yum _____
20 yummy _____
21 think _____
22 soon _____
23 come up to _____
24 knock _____
25 let _____
26 answer _____
27 Not by the hair of my chinny chin chin _____

28 huff _____
29 puff _____
30 blow down _____
31 run away _____
32 the second pig's house _____
33 house of sticks _____
34 the third little pig's house _____
35 the house of bricks _____
36 too . . . to . . . _____
37 strong _____
38 chimney _____
39 climb up _____
40 roof _____
41 get into _____
42 through _____
43 himself _____
44 jump down _____
45 clever _____
46 pot _____
47 boiling water _____
48 fireplace _____
49 splash _____
50 fall into _____
51 scream _____
52 yell _____
53 happily _____
54 ever after _____

B Choose the word that best completes each sentence.

sticks	straw	boiling	hard

1 The first little pig built a house with _____.
2 The second little pig built a house with _____.
3 The third little pig built a house with _____ bricks.
4 The big bad wolf fell into the _____ hot water.

19

Once upon a time, there were _____ little pigs.

One day, they _____ to leave home and make their own houses.

The first little pig built a house with _____.

The second little pig built a house with _____.

The third little pig built a house with hard _____.

In the woods, there lived a big bad _____.

One day, the wolf _____ the first little pig in his house of straw.

"Yum, yum, that pig would be _____,"

thought the big bad wolf.

Soon, the big bad wolf came up to the _____ of straw.

He _____ on the door and said,

"Little pig, little pig, _____ me come in."

The little pig answered,

"No, no! Not by the _____ of my chinny chin chin."

"Then I'll huff, and I'll puff, and I'll _____ your house down,"

said the wolf.

And he huffed and puffed, and he _____ down the house of straw.

The first little pig _____ _____ to the second little pig's house.

He _____ the second little pig about the big bad wolf.

Just _____, the big bad wolf came up to the house of sticks.

He knocked on the _____ and said,

"Little pig, little pig, let me _____ in."

"No, no! Not by the hair of my chinny chin chin," _____

the little pig.

"Then I'll huff, and I'll puff, and I'll blow your house _____,"

said the wolf.

And he _____ and puffed, and he blew down the house of sticks.

The two pigs ran away to the _____ little pig's house.
They told the third little pig _____ the big bad wolf.

Just then, the big bad wolf _____ _____ to the house of bricks.
"Little pig, _____ pig, let me come in," he said.
"No, no! _____ by the hair of my chinny chin chin," answered the little pig.
Then I'll huff, and I'll _____, and I'll blow your house down," said the wolf.
So, the wolf huffed and puffed, and he puffed and _____,
but he _____ blow down the house of bricks.
"My house is too _____ for you to blow down," said the third little pig.

The big bad wolf _____ at the brick house.
He saw a _____ on the top.
"Aha," he _____.
"I will climb up on the _____ and then get into the house through the chimney."
"Then, I can eat the three little pigs," he said to _____.
The big bad wolf _____ down the chimney.

But the third little pig was very _____.
He put a big _____ of boiling water in the fireplace.
SPLASH!
The big bad wolf fell into the _____ hot water.
He _____ and yelled and ran away.
And the three little pigs lived _____ ever after.

A Write the meaning of each word and phrase in Chinese.

1 counting _____

2 skip-counting _____

3 count _____

4 one by one _____

5 by twos _____

6 much faster than _____

7 by ones _____

8 skip-count _____

9 shoes _____

10 find out _____

11 be grouped _____

12 pair _____

13 twelve _____

14 six pairs _____

15 come in _____

16 a pair of eyes _____

17 a pair of arms _____

18 a pair of legs _____

19 wear _____

20 a pair of socks _____

21 a pair of gloves _____

22 a pair of glasses _____

B Choose the word that best completes each sentence.

pairs	counting	wear	skip-count

1 Counting by twos is much faster than _____ by ones.

2 Let's _____ to twenty by twos.

3 Some people _____ a pair of glasses.

4 Many things come in groups of twos, or _____.

Let's count to _____.

One, two, three, four, five, six, seven, _____, nine, ten.

We _____ them one by one.

Let's count them by _____.

Two, four, six, eight, ten.

Counting by twos is much faster than _____ by ones.

When we count _____ twos, we are "skip-counting."

Let's _____ to twenty by twos.

Two, _____, six, eight, ten.

Twelve, fourteen, sixteen, eighteen, _____.

Look at the _____.

Let's _____ _____ how many shoes there are.

They are _____ by twos. We call them a _____.

Can you _____ them by twos?

2, 4, 6, 8, 10, 12.

How _____ shoes are there? There are _____ shoes.

How many _____ of shoes are there? There are _____ pairs of shoes.

Many things come in _____ of twos, or pairs.

You have a pair of _____.

You have a pair of _____.

You have a pair of _____.

People wear a pair of _____.

People wear a pair of _____.

Some people wear a pair of _____.

A Write the meaning of each word and phrase in Chinese.

1 look around _____

2 blue sky _____

3 green grass _____

4 a bunch of _____

5 color _____

6 everywhere _____

7 name _____

8 primary color _____

9 red _____

10 yellow _____

11 blue _____

12 mix _____

13 green _____

14 purple _____

15 orange _____

16 combine _____

17 black _____

18 warm color _____

19 make _____

20 feel excited _____

21 cool color _____

22 feel relaxed _____

23 exciting _____

24 calm _____

B Choose the word that best completes each sentence.

mix	primary	warm	name

1 How many colors can you _____?

2 There are three _____ colors.

3 Red, yellow, and orange are _____ colors.

4 _____ blue and red to make purple.

Listen to the passage and fill in the blanks.

Look _____ you.

Do you see a _____ sky? Some green _____?

A bunch of yellow _____?

We can see _____ everywhere.

How many colors can you _____?

There are three _____ colors.

They are red, _____, and blue.

We can _____ the primary colors together.

Then, we can _____ other colors.

Mix blue and yellow _____. You can make _____.

Mix _____ and red together. You can make _____.

Mix _____ and yellow together. You can make _____.

_____ red, blue, and yellow together.

Then you can make _____.

Some colors are "_____."

Red, yellow, and orange are warm _____.

They make us feel _____ and happy.

Some colors are "_____."

Blue, green, and _____ are cool colors.

They make us feel _____.

Do you like warm, _____ colors?

Or do you like cool, _____ colors?

Musical Instruments and Their Families

A Write the meaning of each word and phrase in Chinese.

1 musical instrument _____
2 family _____
3 look alike _____
4 the same _____
5 keyboard _____
6 organ _____
7 keyboard family _____
8 play _____
9 strike _____
10 key _____
11 string · _____
12 violin _____
13 cello _____
14 viola _____
15 belong to _____

16 string family _____
17 bow _____
18 flute _____
19 clarinet _____
20 woodwind family _____
21 blow _____
22 blow air into _____
23 trumpet _____
24 trombone _____
25 brass family _____
26 xylophone _____
27 triangle _____
28 percussion family _____
29 hit _____
30 stick _____

B Choose the word that best completes each sentence.

| musical | brass | blow | woodwind |

1 There are many _____ instruments.

2 You _____ air into the flute.

3 The flute and clarinet belong to the _____ family.

4 The trumpet and trombone belong to the _____ family.

C **Listen to the passage and fill in the blanks.**

There are many _____ instruments.

Some _____ look alike.

These instruments are in the same _____.

Let's meet the instrument _____.

Do you know any instruments with a _____?

The _____! That's right.

The piano _____ a keyboard.

The _____ also has a keyboard.

They are _____ the keyboard family.

You _____ the keys to play them.

Do you know any instruments with _____?

The violin? The _____? How about the viola?

They all _____ to the string family.

You play them with a _____.

The flute and clarinet belong to the _____ family.

The trumpet and trombone belong to the _____ family.

You _____ air into them to play them.

The drum, xylophone, and triangle belong to _____ family.

You hit them with a _____ to play them.